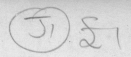

Lily Prior lives in London. An admirer of Italian cuisine and culture, she has travelled extensively in Sicily, where she found the inspiration for *La Cucina*, her first novel. Her most recent novel *Nectar* is also published by Black Swan.

The author invites you to visit her website at www.lilyprior.com

La Cucina

a novel of rapture

LILY PRIOR

BLACK SWAN

LA CUCINA
A BLACK SWAN BOOK : 0 552 99909 1

Published in the US by HarperCollins Publishers Inc.
First publication in Great Britain

PRINTING HISTORY
Black Swan edition published 2001

11 13 15 17 19 20 18 16 14 12

Set in 11/13pt Cochin by
Kestrel Data, Exeter, Devon.

Black Swan Books are published by Transworld Publishers,
61–63 Uxbridge Road, London W5 5SA,
a division of The Random House Group Ltd,
in Australia by Random House Australia (Pty) Ltd,
20 Alfred Street, Milsons Point, Sydney, NSW 2061, Australia,
in New Zealand by Random House New Zealand Ltd,
18 Poland Road, Glenfield, Auckland 10, New Zealand
and in South Africa by Random House (Pty) Ltd,
Endulini, 5a Jubilee Road, Parktown 2193, South Africa.

Printed and bound in Great Britain by
Clays Ltd, St Ives plc.

FOR MY MOTHER, JANET

I would like to thank my husband, Christopher, who never fails to inspire and encourage me. Without him this book would never have been written. I would also like to thank my agent, Jean Naggar, for her faith in me and *La Cucina*, her invaluable support, her hard work, and her kindness. And I would like to thank my editor, Julia Serebrinsky, for her inspired thoughts on the manuscript. Finally, I would like to thank all of you who encouraged me and helped me along the way.

CONTENTS

THE CHARACTERS OF MY STORY

Guglielmo Calzino

Lorenzo Calzino
*Brothers to
Donna Isabella
Fiore, my uncles*

Pietro Calzino

Rosario, the half-witted farmhand

Luciano, the shepherd

Don Umberto Sogno, Bartolomeo's father, a man of honour

Donna Evangelina Sogno, Bartolomeo's mother

Gallo Carlo, the cockerel

Donna Rubino Sogno (Nonna Sogno), Bartolomeo's paternal
  grandmother

Donna Sophia Bacci, Bartolomeo's fiancée

Don Fredo Bacci, friend of Don Umberto Sogno, a man of
  honour

Donna Theresa Bacci, Sophia's mother

Ernesto Tombi, the undertaker in Castiglione

Donna Ginevra Bacci

Donna Perla Bacci

Donna Margarita Bacci
*Bartolomeo's
five sisters*

Donna Lucia Bacci

Donna Anna Bacci

Barese and Pirone, henchmen of Don Umberto Sogno

Signor Raimondo Bandiera, director of the Biblioteca
  Nationale

Signora Bandiera, his fragrant wife

Quinto Cavallo, the goldsmith

Signor Rivoli, the bank manager and a Peeping Tom

Signora Rossi, wife of Crocifisso the doorman

Restituto Raimondo, the one-eyed doorman who succeeds
  Crocifisso

Balbina Burgondofara, dairymaid, and Antonino Calabrese's
  mistress

The widow Palumbo, friend of Don Sergio Frolla

Biancamaria Ossobuco, the twins' consort

Banquo Cuniberto, the tailor in Castiglione

Dr Leobino, the Fiore family doctor

Little Rosa

Rosita   *My nieces*

Rosina

La Cucina

PROLOGUE

I lie luxuriantly on the table, the cool, silky oak sticking to my naked flesh. Rump, thighs, plump. This night is the culmination, the final lesson. By the light of the candles I stretch out and watch l'Inglese as he moves gently among the shadows on the far side of the kitchen, the clattering of his pans punctuated occasionally by the sounds of the summer night, the buzzing of a mosquito, the braying of a mule.

L'Inverno

THE WINTER

CHAPTER ONE

Tip the flour in a heap on the table. The old oak table, legacy of Nonna Calzino, smoothed to a brilliant lustre by all the years of daily use. Not too much flour. Not too little. Just the right amount. Fine flour milled from durum wheat by Papa Grazzi at Mascali. Sprinkle in some sea salt, a good measure. Add some fresh eggs and some extra egg yolks, sufficient for the amount of flour, and also some good olive oil and a very little cold water.

Using your fingers, mix the liquids into the flour, combining your ingredients until a smooth paste is formed. The eggs may feel slimy to the touch but this is natural. Knead well, using the heels of the hands in a forward, downward movement.

Knead just until the arms begin to ache and the small bead of sweat starts to trace its way down the spine from somewhere between the shoulder blades to the cleft between the buttocks. This, of course, in winter; in summer the sweat pours down the face and neck, dampening the clothes and making droplets on the table and the flagstone floor.

When the dough is smooth and elastic, brush it with a little oil, cover it with a damp cloth, and leave it to rest, for it too is fatigued. While you are waiting for your dough to relax you can leaf through the pages of a magazine, observing this season's latest fashions, or gaze from the window at young Maria flirting with the postman on the street corner below. Look at Fredo riding by on his bicycle, or at the pack of stray dogs escaping from the dog catcher, and at life in general passing you by.

Then you may begin the rolling. Dust the table lightly with flour and divide your dough into eight equal pieces. Taking one piece, begin by moving the rolling pin in a motion away from you, pressing evenly to create a rectangular shape. Continue thus until your sheet of pasta is long and thin and about the thickness of the blade of a knife. The knife that slit Bartolomeo's throat. Slicing through his beautiful young flesh like a *coltello* through lard.

Cut the sheet in half horizontally and hang it over a pole to dry for five minutes. Repeat with the remaining pieces of dough to make sixteen sheets. Slice carefully the length of each sheet, forming the thinnest strips you can. Again let these dry on the pole for another five minutes. Here you have your spaghetti, which, with a delicious sauce of ripe tomatoes, basil, sleek aubergine, and ricotta you will eat for lunch, when office workers, acrobats, and slaughtermen return home for the siesta and for a few brief hours the restless city sleeps.

Following the murder of Bartolomeo, I made pasta night and day. I retreated into the kitchen in the same way that some women retreat into convents, as Pasquala Tredici did after her sweetheart, Roberto, was gored to death by a bull.

I had always loved my food: in those dark days it was all that could give me comfort. I did not emerge from my self-imposed exile in *la cucina* for a long time. I assuaged my grief by cooking, and cooking, and cooking some more.

At that time I was still living with my family on the farm in the Alcantara valley beneath the citadel of Castiglione, on the far eastern side of the island of Sicily, near the slopes of the great volcano.

The valley of the Alcantara is an area famous for its fruitfulness. Its olives are more succulent, its oranges juicier, its pigs porkier than in any other region. The abundance of our land is reflected in our people, who, as a general rule, are wholesome, hearty, and strong.

The virility of our men and the fecundity of our women have also been noted; families tend to be large here, and the urge to mate is strong among both humans and animals.

By a strange phenomenon multiple births are as common among Alcantara women as they are among sows; we give birth to many twins, triplets, even quadruplets, and identical little faces fill the classrooms in the local school. We are so accustomed to seeing duplicates and triplicates of farmhands, housewives, and goatherds that they fail even to draw notice, except among strangers. But few strangers come here.

In our lush valley, they say the fire in the loins of the

inhabitants draws flame from the smouldering mountain that dominates our skyline. It casts its spell over the lives brewing in its shadow, where for millions of years it has ejaculated its own life force, clothing its slopes in rich black lava.

CHAPTER TWO

To begin at the beginning, my name is Rosa Fiore. I am
of the Fiores, an ancient family that has lived here in
Sicily, it is said, since the time of the Greeks.

My family was made up of my parents, Madre and
Padre Fiore, and, until my ninth year, my six older
brothers: Luigi, Leonardo, Mario, Giuliano, Giuseppe,
and Salvatore. When I was eight my younger brothers,
Guerra and Pace, came along.

My family was, I suppose, a typical Sicilian family:
large and loud.

My mother, Isabella Fiore, was a small but formidable
woman who ruled over the *fattoria* like the avenging angel
that looks down from the frieze on the front of the Chiesa
di San Pietro. Everyone was scared of her. Papa said her
black eyes could spit venom like an asp, though I never
saw her do this.

My papa was large and bluff and terrified of Mama.
Dear Papa. I never saw him without his mountain cap,
even indoors; he even took baths in it, though I have to
admit that he bathed infrequently. He even wore it in

bed, in case of fire during the night or, more likely, an eruption of the volcano. Papa also wore a large mustard plaster on the back of his neck his entire adult life to cover a suppurating boil that would never heal.

When I was twelve Papa disappeared. But wait, I am getting ahead of myself.

Mama and Papa never once spoke a word to each other, not where I could hear them. They maintained an arch distance from one another while retaining an unquenchable desire for the pleasures of the other's flesh. This desire was so strong that they were often found engaged in a frenzied coupling in the hayloft, the cowshed, or the fields. It wasn't until I became an adult that I realized what they had been doing. As a girl I was as innocent as a lark, like Mama intended me to be. So the numerous occasions when I came upon them fucking one another senseless didn't register with me until much, much later.

After the hungry dragon that lived inside her loins was satisfied, albeit briefly, Mama would adjust her skirts. She would treat Papa to a look of utter disdain which never failed to paralyse him, speeding the demise of his already dwindling member. Having done so, Mama would return to the unending duties of a farmer's wife.

From this happy union, when I was eight years old, came my twin brothers, Guerra and Pace, War and Peace.

On the night of their birth, an inflamed moon hung low over the valley, and the local people gathered by its light outside the *fattoria*. They came because they heard rumours that an unnatural birth was taking place at the home of the Fiores. This was heralded that morning on the neighbouring farm, where a pig with two tails was born, a sure sign that the balance of nature has been disturbed.

It is true that in recent weeks, Mama's belly had swelled so much that even the brood mare in the lower paddock eyed her with pity. She was certainly carrying more than one child; possibly even more than two, although, of course, this was not unusual for our valley.

The crowd waited eagerly for news, passing round a flask of grappa to keep out the cold. They breathed on their frigid fingers to warm them up, creating puffs of vapour all around. In the distance the volcano rumbled its curse, and the word went round that Isabella Fiore was about to give birth to a monster.

Some of the more pious clutched rosaries and whispered fervent prayers while others lit torches to ward off evil spirits.

Inside the house, my brothers and I were kept shut in *la cucina* and told to play in front of the fire. We knew something strange was happening but we were not allowed to know what it was. It is curious how, as children, we sense taboos; we instinctively know what we are allowed to question and what we are not supposed to mention. The boys sat around playing poker and occasionally fighting while I baked a batch of honey biscuits to calm my eight-year-old nerves.

Suddenly, while I was stirring the walnuts into the boiling honey, a piercing scream reverberated through the night air. It was followed by another and another still. We all looked around in fear.

Outside, some of the villagers were forced to cover their ears, so loud was the din and so pitiful the cries.

The screaming went on and on. All the biscuits had been baked and eaten and we had fallen asleep in the glow of the fire when a scream louder than the ones preceding it made everything silent. The scream roused me with a start, causing me to fall from my little chair to the floor. I looked out through the crack in the door at the crowd gathered in the yard and saw the townsfolk crossing themselves in one movement.

Nearest to me, I heard one woman say: 'Isabella Fiore is dead for sure; no woman, however resolute, could survive such a labour and tortuous birth.'

Her neighbour nodded her agreement and crossed herself again.

What did it all mean? I asked myself. None of it made any sense. Instinctively I began to knead some dough. Nothing has ever comforted me so much as pounding away with my fists at a warm and elastic mixture.

Then the silence was broken by the cries of one baby, and then another one joined in.

At least it was a live birth, some of the women in the crowd mumbled. Heaven be praised; the cries were said to resemble those of a human creature.

Before long the head of Margarita Gengiva, the tooth-less midwife who attended at births in the region, emerged from an upstairs window.

'It's a monster,' she screamed through her soft gums, spraying those beneath with a burst of saliva in her excitement.

Over the din of the baying crowd she delivered her masterstroke:

'It is a thing with two heads, one body, two arms, and three legs.'

With that she waved her kerchief in a defiant gesture at those assembled and retreated inside. She closed the window behind her with a bang.

By the grace of the archangel Gabriel, a thing with two heads and one body!

Following a hurried meeting of the elders, the boldest in the crowd, who also happened to be the most inebriated, formed a deputation. They crossed the farmyard as one and proceeded to the house to insist that the monster's throat be slit and its corpse burnt on a pyre to prevent the spread of evil spirits throughout the region.

The priest, Padre Francesco, appeared on the steps at the front of the house to calm the crowd. He made the sign of the cross and uttered a benediction:

'*Benedicat et custodiat nos omnipotens et misericors Dominus, Pater, et Filius, et Spiritus Sanctus*. Amen.'

'Amen,' responded the faithful and unfaithful alike.

'These little babes are no more a monster than I am . . .' he said.

Some of those who had enjoyed too much wine nudged one another and chortled.

'Take them to your hearts, good people, for they are as much in need of God's love as yourselves.'

'Aye, Padre, but when my wine is all turned sour in its barrels,' said Fuscolo Bancale.

'When my flocks stray and lose themselves on the mountain,' added Sperato Maddaloni.

'When my cheese goes rancid in the dairy,' said Mafalda Pruneto.

'When my olives mildew,' said Sesto Fissaggi.

'. . . Then we'll know it is a judgement upon us for allowing devils disguised as babes into our midst,' concluded Fuscolo, turning his one angry eye in the direction of the priest.

'Aye, the good Lord preserve us from devils and evil spirits,' added Mafalda.

'Holy Mother protect us from monsters and goblins,' said Sperato.

The talk and imprecations continued as dawn broke and eventually the crowd dispersed into the shadows.

CHAPTER THREE

In the village, an explanation was sought and speculation abounded. Nothing like this had ever been seen before. It wasn't long before Mama and Papa's morals were questioned by all.

There was talk of Papa's foul couplings with a sow. Some accused him of philanderings with fairies.

Mama fared even worse. Had Giacomo Meletti not seen her mating with a ram? Or was it a sheep? Further exotic reports suggested an antelope or a water buffalo, but these possibilities were discounted by the more sensible folk who pointed out that none of these creatures were known to inhabit the region. And if they did, none had been seen except by the garrulous and not entirely reliable altar boy Donatello Mancini.

Mama's relationship with Padre Francesco, the parish priest, was also called into question. Had they not been caught in the campanile swinging from the bell ropes? In flagrante on the high altar itself? Could the birth be a judgement on the couple for flouting the canons of clerical celibacy and marital fidelity? Should the bishop be informed about this?

Mama was also accused, wrongly, I am sure, by some of the more vicious-minded town gossips of oedipal couplings with her sons Luigi, Leonardo, Mario, Giuliano, Giuseppe, and Salvatore.

There was so much gossip that I couldn't even recall the details, until I was forced to live through it again many years later. But I am getting ahead of myself again.

Whatever the cause of the judgement, for judgement it certainly was, the result was all too plain to behold: a monster with two heads and one body had been delivered of Isabella Fiore.

Even Mama's constitutional sang-froid was shaken visibly on beholding the fruits of her womb for the first time. At first she thought she was hallucinating, either due to the pain experienced during labour or the evil cocktail of drugs dispensed by Margarita Gengiva, the midwife.

'Jesus, what the fuck is that?' she cried.

'It's a baby that's gone a little bit wrong,' I replied, having finally been allowed upstairs to see my baby brothers.

Grappling with the ungainly form of the twins wrapped in a blanket I asked with all seriousness:

'Are you quite sure you put the right ingredients into the mixture, Mama?'

Papa hung his head in shame. He could not feel entirely blameless for the tragedy. Still, it was not his nature to brood, and before long he had sold an expurgated version of the story of the twins' birth to

32

La Sicilia, Catania's main newspaper, complete with photographs, which brought him a brief moment of fame and some hundreds of lire.

Unfortunately the publicity generated by this feature in the newspaper led to the attempted kidnapping of the twins by the gypsies of the Circo Veneziano, whose purpose, it appears, was to exhibit them in a travelling sideshow and charge admission. The attempt was foiled, I am proud to say, thanks to my unwavering vigilance.

On the day in question I was sitting out on the step watching the boys, who were asleep in their cot, when two strange men came into the yard. They were dressed in parti-coloured hose with ruffles and flounces and shiny shoes and pointy hats and were quite unlike any men I had ever seen on the farm.

I stared long at them as they approached.

'Who are you?' I charged them boldly.

'Don't be afraid. We've come to take the little ones away. Your mama says it's all right to. Come on now, hand them over.'

'I will not,' I replied defiantly.

One of them reached over to take the cot. Quickly I bit a sizable chunk from his hand. He jumped up and down with pain as blood dripped onto the ground and he used words that I had never heard before (Mama didn't allow cursing in the kitchen).

I took hold of the cot and began to shout for help. This woke the twins, who added the strength of their disgruntled voices to mine.

Undeterred, the second man tried to wrestle the cot

away from me, but I hung on to it with my little fingers, screaming all the while.

At long last Papa emerged from the cowshed still fastening his trousers while at the same time brandishing a pitchfork. He charged at the men, who fled at the sight of the shiny prongs.

From then on we never let the babies out of our sight for a second, and for a long time afterwards I saw the horrid brightly coloured men in my dreams. I have never visited the circus.

Mama, regrettably, could never quite overcome her feelings of repulsion towards the twins. And so I became almost a mother to the hideous little creatures, remaking the baby clothes I had knitted while Mama was pregnant, and changing their nappies.

CHAPTER FOUR

When I was twelve, Padre Fiore disappeared.

It was not uncommon in Sicily in those days for people to disappear. Their bodies were never found. They formed the foundations of new roads or railway tracks or buildings, were hidden in disused wells or mine shafts; some were chopped up and fed to dogs; others were dissolved in baths of acid.

Such disappearances were known as *lupara bianca*, or 'white deaths': a way for the Mafia to dispose of people who had become inconvenient, dangerous, or embarrassing.

Lupara bianca were particularly distressing for the relatives, largely because it was so difficult to determine whether the loved one had simply disappeared on his own, or whether he had been forcibly disappeared. You couldn't be sure. A niggling doubt would never go away completely.

For some days Mama resolutely refused to believe that Papa had disappeared. There had been some mistake, she said; he had no connection with the Mafia. But after a week she was forced to accept what everyone else had known all along: that he had gone and would not be coming back. I knew he was dead; he would never separate voluntarily from his mountain cap, which I found in the yard on the day of his disappearance.

Despite the fact that there was no body, Mama arranged a lavish burial, and arrayed us all in black for the occasion. The twins, then aged four, were decked out in a three-legged suit of knickerbockers with matching tricorn hats and were cajoled into trotting alongside the coffin as a sort of mascot. They shed no tears.

For appearance's sake, Mama screamed with a grief she could not feel, and in an impressive display even managed to collapse at the graveside in a well-received show of anguish behind a thickly veiled hat.

Luigi, Leonardo, Mario, Giuliano, Giuseppe, and Salvatore acted as pallbearers and still managed to crack jokes; I clutched the mountain cap in my fist and all alone grieved for my papa.

Life went on, however, and within three months suitors were being received at the *fattoria*, for Mama was a wealthy widow and one who, according to local legend, was able to satisfy more than a man's pockets.

Rehearsals were held during the long, hot summer of 1927. With all the elder boys out working the fields, Guerra and Pace and I were sent out of the way when the suitors came.

The suitors were put through a trial run according to a strict timetable: morning, afternoon, and evening. When their time was up they would emerge from the *fattoria* bathed in sweat, dabbing at their brows with handkerchiefs and adjusting their rumpled clothing.

We would sit on the gate and watch them come and go: the judge, the councillor, the pharmacist, the candle-maker. All were given a fair shot.

Then, one Wednesday morning during the school holidays, a new suitor came to call: he was a stranger to the region, and was much younger than any of his predecessors; he was even younger than Mama.

As usual Mama shooed me and the little ones out of the house before admitting the man inside. This time, however, something unusual happened. We soon began to hear noises coming from the house: the sound of ripping cloth first, and then furniture scraping across the floor or being thrown across the room; strange banging noises filled the air along with squeaking and thumping sounds; then human sounds added to the din: groans, grunts, cries, and finally screams.

Mama had not made so much noise since the night of the twins' birth four years earlier. I was frightened, it is true, but I could not let the little ones see it, so we continued with our play and tried to block from our ears the clamour that was coming from the house.

At one especially loud burst of cries the twins ran across to the window and peered inside. They were nimble on their three little legs and could run quite fast. I just could not catch them in time.

'No, boys, you must not look,' I said, but it was too late to stop them.

With their little noses smudging the glass they could see a strange four-legged creature writhing on the table in the front parlour.

At first they thought it was a fellow creature: one like themselves with the wrong number of legs, a strange torso, and no real place in the world.

When the mist created by their breath on the glass diminished they could see that part of the creature was their mama, without clothes on, and the other part was the man who had crossed the yard and entered the house a little while ago.

They were still trying to register all this when they were spotted by Mama and waved away from the window with the kind of angry gesture that is used to shoo flies.

Unlike the previous suitors, this one stayed a long time. The screams and crashes continued throughout the morning, afternoon, and into the evening. All day long we waited in the yard for the time when we would be readmitted into the house. The twins grew bored with play and occupied themselves with tracing patterns in the dust with their three little feet. Their etchings showed the writhing monster they had seen through the window.

As the sun went down I crept into *la cucina* to prepare supper for the older boys and the unmarried farmhands who sometimes ate at the *fattoria*.

A scene of devastation met my eyes.

Chairs were overturned and several were even broken; a barrel of ale had been turned over and flooded the floor with suds; the shelves had collapsed, smashing every jar of preserves I had so lovingly prepared; plates were broken, the dresser drawers had been pulled out, and their contents were spewed all over the room. The earthenware water jars lined up along the sink were smashed, the huge kettle was on its side, and the fire had gone out.

I set about tidying things up, and soon had the fire lit and the food cooking before bathing the twins in the sink and singing them to sleep.

That night as I sat with my brothers Luigi, Leonardo, Mario, Giuliano, Giuseppe, and Salvatore and the farm-hands at the long table having supper, Mama and her new suitor appeared in *la cucina* without a hint of em-barrassment. He looked as exhausted as it was possible to look. Mama, by contrast, was radiant. She looked seven-teen again.

'My children, this is Antonino Calabrese,' she said. 'From now on he will be living here and will be your new father.'

Antonino Calabrese, it appeared, had passed the test.

Four months after the funeral, a wedding procession that started at the *fattoria* wound its way up through the steep streets of Castiglione to the Chiesa di San Antonio Abate.

This time the twins were done out in a white sailor suit but they skipped along less jauntily than on the previous occasion. Mama became Signora Calabrese and Signor Calabrese became a wealthy young man.

CHAPTER FIVE

La cucina is the heart of the *fattoria*, and has formed the backdrop to the lives of our family, the Fiores, as far back as, and further than, anyone can remember. This kitchen has witnessed our joys, griefs, births, deaths, nuptials, and fornications for hundreds of years.

Even now the ghosts of our forebears gather in the kitchen, sitting around like old friends, participating in discussions and passing judgement on the activities of the living.

La cucina bears the scents of its past, and every event in its history is recorded with an olfactory memorandum. Here vanilla, coffee, nutmeg, and confidences; there the milky-sweet smell of babies, old leather, sheep's cheese, and violets. In the corner by the larder hangs the stale tobacco smell of old age and death, while the salty scent of lust and satiation clings to the air by the cellar steps along with the aroma of soap, garlic, beeswax, lavender, jealousy, and disappointment.

La cucina runs along the entire length of the rear of the farmhouse. Along one wall is the huge fireplace containing the various ovens for baking, and a number of open fires. Above these hangs the collection of roasting spits and fire-blackened kettles and cauldrons.

The walls of the kitchen are discoloured by wood smoke and the grease from suckling pigs, and are now a rich sepia, which is reflected in the hue of the mellow flagstones of the floor. The windows are small and placed high up to keep the kitchen cool in the sweet, hot days of summer and warm in the depths of winter, when snow lies deep on the slopes of the volcano in the distance and the frozen farmhands come in after a long day in the fields to drink a cup of Mama's strong ale.

In the centre of the kitchen is a huge oak table that has been in our family since the days of Pasquale Fiore, the pirate; it was said to have been constructed from the wrecked remains of the deck of his ship, *La Duchessa*, which was washed up on the shore just south of Taormina after the cataclysmic storm in which he and his pirate band perished.

I was born on this very table. On the day of my birth, back in the summer of 1915, Mama was making *sfincione* for lunch, and as she kneaded the dough her waters broke. She was alone in the *fattoria*, for Papa and the elder boys were out working in the fields furthest from the house, and there was no-one to summon help or to give assistance.

Mama hauled herself onto the table and before the dough had time to prove, she had delivered me on her own, severing the umbilical cord with the same knife with which she had been filleting anchovies moments before.

On opening my tiny lips to scream I revealed a full set

of teeth, with a large gap between the two front ones. This was interpreted as a good omen. It was said that Rosa Fiore would be lucky.

My passion for cooking seems to have stemmed from the circumstances of my birth. Even as a stocky tot I was always to be found in the kitchen, learning my art and preparing doll-sized feasts in my miniature pots and pans.

It was also on this table that every departed member of the Fiore clan was laid out in his best clothes to accept the last respects of family, friends, and neighbours before making his final journey to the cemetery on the hill.

When Nonno Fiore died he was set upon the table according to tradition, and on the morning of his funeral I fed the corpse with some freshly fried *panelle*, the delicious chickpea fritters I did so well, believing they would restore my Nonno to life. I was disappointed, however, to discover that the *panelle* could not resurrect the dead. For a fleeting moment my faith in food was shaken. Nonno Fiore was buried with the grease still clinging to his whiskers, his toothless mouth bulging with food.

CHAPTER SIX

It was not unnatural then for me to take refuge in *la cucina* following the tragedy, but no-one was able to anticipate the scale of my culinary catharsis.

I began by preparing pasta: my deft little fingers forming the intricate shapes of rigatoni, ravioli, spiralli, spaghetti, cannelloni, and linguini. Then I would brew sauces of sardines, or anchovies or zucchini or sheep's cheeses, of saffron, pine nuts, currants, and fennel. These I would simmer in the huge iron cauldrons which were constantly bubbling above the fire. My pasta dishes, I have to say, were famous throughout the province, and the scent of my sauces carried by the breeze was sufficient to fill a poor man's stomach.

I also kneaded bread and produced the finest *pane rimacinato*, the most delicious *ciabbata* and *focaccia* that had ever been tasted in the region. Sometimes I would add wild thyme to the dough, or fragrant rosemary, plucked fresh from the hedgerow, with the dew still on the leaves.

The velvety texture of my breads could be produced

only by the most thorough kneading, and soon I developed biceps and quadriceps to match those of any of the farmhands, while my pectoral muscles expanded to augment the already generous proportions of my breasts.

Late one night, as I pounded the dough, the thumps of my nocturnal thrusts disturbed the other occupants of the *fattoria*, Luigi in his solitary lovemaking and Mama and Antonino Calabrese in their conjugal bliss.

Mama rushed from her bed, leaving her young husband withering, fearing that Lui had again managed to sneak that whore from the *locanda* at Linguaglossa into his room. At any other time she would have beaten him around the head for his sins, but on this occasion she was relieved to discover that he was enjoying the pleasures of the flesh alone.

Mama flew along the corridor with nightgown gaping and feet bare to ensure that no venal sin was taking place under her roof, a sin which was likely to jeopardize the eternal salvation of her only daughter and her other seven sons.

She found the twins, Guerra and Pace, still sleeping soundly on the mattress in their little cupboard. Leonardo, Mario, Giuliano, Giuseppe, and Salvatore were quaking under the bedclothes fearing an imminent eruption of the volcano.

'Rosa, *figlia mia*, come to bed,' Mama said wearily as she entered the kitchen to discover me at work with my brawny forearms preparing yet another batch of dough.

'Later, Mama, later,' I replied, although in truth I could barely stand without supporting myself on the table, such was my exhaustion.

And yet my kneading, exhausting though it was, brought me relief like nothing else, and my fatigue purified me, bathing me in a rarefied feeling of calm.

I produced bread of such quality in such quantity that Paolo Alboni, the *panettiere* in the town, feared I would put him out of business. When our family and our neighbours, friends and distant relatives throughout Catania Province could eat no more, I was forced to give the bread away, leaving it on a makeshift table on the main road to Randazzo, so that pilgrims could nourish themselves when passing by. Soon a long line of the poor and needy was gathering at the kitchen door of the *fattoria* awaiting my bounty, only to be shooed away, and if they were persistent, beaten by Mama.

In time I had spent all my savings, the savings that were to have paid for my trousseau, on flour and other ingredients, and once my savings were gone, then I started to borrow, driving the cart to Randazzo to secure the necessary provisions on the black market, paying an escalated price and falling prey to the town's many usurers.

It was not only pasta and bread that I made out of my grief. I brewed tomato sauce in a quantity so immense it could vie with the output of Pronto's Pomodoro factory at Fiumefreddo, which was at that time subject to a protection racket run by the Mafia.

One morning I discovered the severed head of one of the sheepdogs outside the back door with a note attached advising me to cease production of tomato sauce if I did not wish to damage the sender's business and risk his displeasure. I recognized this as a warning from the

Mafia, and yet it did not worry me; I was beyond worrying about man-made threats at this stage. And so I threw the dog's head in the fire and turned my attention to preserving instead.

For two months I bottled oranges and apricots, peaches and pears, raspberries and nectarines, plums and figs in a rich sugar syrup laced with lemon zest.

I pickled olives and cucumbers in brine, and packed mushrooms, pepperoni, artichokes, and asparagus in jars with olive oil.

I made jams and preserves of berries and fruits, which then lined the shelves on the walls in the cellar, each one labelled in my own hand and bearing the date of my agony.

Once the supply of fresh fruit and vegetables had become exhausted, I turned my attention to Mama's home-reared livestock.

First I slaughtered the pigs, even my pet, Miele, which looked up at me with tiny, doleful eyes, clearly doubting that I had it in me to end his life with my cleaver. He was wrong; I was beyond compassion now. As I wielded my knife I felt, albeit temporarily, my anger slipping away, and for a few brief moments I was calm.

I slit the throat of each pig and collected the blood in buckets to make into sausages, which would later be served with a garnish of fennel seeds.

Next I cured bacon and hams, which hung on hooks in the cool larder, and then I made pies and meatballs, ragù, rich pâtés and succulent roasts. My hands were, I recall, for a period of some weeks streaked with blood, as was sometimes my face, and I would wear a blood-soaked apron in the manner of a *macellaio*. It pleased me to go about like this: somewhat wild and dangerous, and bearing on my body the sign of the blood that was weeping from my heart.

When I was done with the pigs, I wrung the necks of the chickens, so that none remained to lay any eggs, and Luigi was urgently dispatched to the market at Randazzo to buy a box of chicks together with three or four mature hens to provide *uovi* for Antonino Calabrese's breakfast.

The *pollo alla Messinese*, a sumptuous dish of chicken smothered in a tuna-flavoured mayonnaise that I produced, would have fed three hundred guests at a wedding. Unfortunately there was to be no wedding.

Following the chicken incident, Mama banned me from slaughtering any more animals, so I turned to the dairy instead.

I made salty ricotta by boiling sheep's milk with salt and skimming the whey with a bunch of twigs in the old tradition, just as Nonna Fiore had taught me. The ricotta too I made in great quantities, storing it in barrels in the roof of the cowshed.

Eventually Mama came to the end of her patience. The farm could not produce harvests to keep pace with my cooking; pasta and bread were going to waste, for no-one could be found to eat them and the farmhands had grown fat and lazy through overeating; not a single fruit or vegetable remained in store, the oil and vinegar barrels were empty, only the sheep were left, for the pigs had all been slaughtered, together with the chickens, in what seemed to Mama like a killing frenzy. The discovery of Boli the sheepdog's carcass decomposed in a ditch seemed even more sinister. The dripping of ricotta from the roof of the cowshed was equally upsetting, and the more superstitious of the farmhands suspected the presence of the devil and refused to go inside.

Mama gathered her family around her: my brothers Luigi, Leonardo, Mario, Giuliano, Giuseppe, and Salvatore, the twins, Guerra and Pace, and her young husband, Antonino Calabrese. Luigi was sent to summon me into the parlour, but I refused to leave the kitchen.

'Mama, she won't come,' I heard Lui reporting back to the gathering in the parlour. 'She says she is too busy making *dolci*, the *cassata*, *cannoli*, and *torta di ricotta*.'

Undeterred, Mama led her little procession along the passage and into the kitchen.

'Rosa,' Mama began, 'this cannot go on. You must cease this unending *cucina*.'

I said nothing, but that same day I packed my few things in my suitcase, and taking from the hook on the wall the cage containing my parrot, Celeste, I left Castiglione for Palermo.

My family fed upon my heartache for many, many years. During the war, when food was in short supply, my grief ensured that ours was the only family in the region that did not experience some hunger.

What had at first seemed to Mama a curse had become a blessing, and she thanked the good Lord for it at High Mass every Sunday.

The hams were served at the celebrations to mark Luigi's wedding to the barmaid from Linguaglossa, which was more years than I can remember after the death of Bartolomeo and my departure. As my brothers' children were growing up, it was not unusual to see them feasting on apricots or artichokes from a barrel or bottle they had found, dating from the time of their Aunt Rosa's tragedy.

CHAPTER SEVEN

Having prepared my lunch of *pasta alla Norma*, I left my little apartment for my job at the Biblioteca Nationale in the city centre. As I climbed the steps circling the central interior I looked around the building where I had sold the last twenty-five years of my life. I was due to receive my commemorative plate this year, inscribed with my name and years of service, in a presentation given by the director.

I had gained a lot of weight since I left the *fattoria* twenty-five years ago. My breasts, still large, now sagged, and in a few years more would sink further to reach what remained of my waist. My hair, once the colour and lustre of a raven, was streaked with grey, and years of cataloguing books in the library had weakened my eyesight so that I balanced a pair of severe spectacles on the bridge of my nose.

It is not right to think that I had lived in grief for all of these years. Honestly, once I had emerged from *la cucina* at Castiglione, my rage left me. In fact, I felt nothing for a quarter of a century. I did not even continue to mourn

50

the loss of Bartolomeo. I accepted my life, and it caused me no pain.

I had come here, to the library, on the very first day I arrived on the autobus from Castiglione with my parrot and my tiny suitcase in my hand, to make a new life in the big city, away from the town where I had been born and grew up and where everyone knew my business.

In Palermo I had no past; no-one knew me, my family, or my tragedy. All they knew was what I told them, and being from Catania Province, I told them very little.

Back on that winter day in 1933, the rain fell desultorily as I disembarked from the autobus at the Capolinea in the centre of Palermo. Not knowing where to go, I spent the whole day walking around the Arab quarter, thinking how best to find work and how I would survive in the noise and bustle and confusion that was unlike anything I had ever experienced. Even on my infrequent trips to Randazzo, the most substantial town in my region, I had never felt so anonymous and alone in the din of surrounding humanity.

On passing the *biblioteca*, I noticed a handwritten sign on one of the glass-covered notice boards that advertised the position of a clerk for a reasonable salary.

I mustered my courage and went inside. After I made the necessary enquiries about the job – it mostly involved shelving books – and left the parrot and my suitcase in the care of Crocifisso the doorman, I was invited into the office of the senior librarian. He seemed pleased with my answers to his questions, and proposed that I start the next day. My salary of twenty lire a week was subject to a probationary period of one month.

I left the library in high spirits, congratulating myself on my courage. Then I set myself the task of finding a place to live. Again fate seemed to smile upon me. A little further down the Corso Vittorio Emanuele, I came upon a grocer's shop that also bore a sign in its window: ROOMS TO LET, RESPECTABLE PERSONS ONLY, EIGHT LIRE PER WEEK.

The grocer, Donna Maria Frolla, was a little old lady, at least eighty years old. She sat behind a counter framed with prosciutto, salami, all manner of cheeses, *ciabatta*, fresh pastas, panettone, and *biscotti*. Donna Frolla assessed me with her squinty eyes while petting a fat black pug sitting on her lap.

'*Prego*, signorina?'

'Signora, I have come about the rooms,' I stuttered.

Donna Frolla viewed me with mistrust through her one level eye.

'Are you married?' she asked without any pre-liminaries. 'For the rooms are only suitable for single occupancy.'

'No, I'm not married,' I replied as the knife twisted in my wound.

'So what are you wanting lodgings for?' the grocer continued. 'I keep a respectable house, signorina, I wasn't looking to take a single girl into the rooms.'

'I work at the library, signora, and am looking for a place close by. I live quietly and can promise I will cause you no trouble.'

At this the *negoziante* softened, for she had a great respect for learning and books, and would be proud to be able to tell her customers when they came in to buy their coffee that she had rented her rooms to a librarian.

Donna Frolla left the shop in the care of her husband, who was even older and more shrunken than herself, picked up the pug in her arms, and led me, my parrot, and my suitcase along the Corso Vittorio Emanuele to the duomo. She took a left turn into a little narrow street, Via Vicolo Brugno, crisscrossed with lines of laundry.

At number fifty-three, she took a key from her pocket and admitted me to the rooms on the second floor. There was a reasonably sized kitchen, a bedroom with a small balcony, and a shared bathroom. It was a little dark, a little fetid, but I needed a roof over my head and did not want to be back out there pacing the streets among strangers in search of something better.

After Signora Frolla left I opened the doors onto the balcony and looked out. The street was so narrow there was only an arm's length between the balconies on my side of the street and those on the other. How different it was from the majestic view from the windows of my room at the *fattoria*, where the eye roved over an expanse of lush green fields to the white-dusted volcano in the far distance.

This is how I started my new life and a career as a shelver. After years of hard work I attained my present position of assistant junior librarian, and I've been as content as one would expect of a woman in my predicament.

I knew that the younger girls in the library derided me. They mimicked my country accent, and laughed at my homemade clothes, in particular at my grey and

capacious underwear, which I once accidentally revealed
to the merciless Costanza while taking off my winter
boots with an over-vigorous motion of the legs.

They mocked my passion for food, my generous size,
my overwhelming breasts.

Most of all they ridiculed me for not having a man, and
behind my back, and sometimes even to my face, they
called me *la zitella*, the spinster, and *la vergine*.

But I was not a virgin. I knew what it was to experience the love of a man, in spite of all Mama's efforts
to make sure that I did not.

From an early age Mama would lock me in my room
at night, fearing for my virtue in a house full of men,
and by day she kept a vigilant eye on the lustful Luigi,
his brothers Leonardo, Mario, Giuliano, Giuseppe, and
Salvatore, and even the unfortunate twins, Guerra
and Pace, and also the farmhands, the postman, the
priest, Padre Francesco, and in their time both her
husbands: poor Papa and his successor, Antonino
Calabrese. She trusted no man between the stages of
pubescence and senescence, for Mama knew men, and
she did not like what she saw in them.

Nevertheless, I have known love and I still remember,
decades later, the one night with Bartolomeo that
changed the course of my life for ever.

It was, I recall quite clearly, the very hot summer of
1932, the year of the mysterious, some said supernatural,
rain of toads on the slopes of the volcano.

Mama had taken the unprecedented step of staying for
one night away from home. Her mother, my grandmother, Nonna Calzino, was dying of haemorrhoids in

Adrano, which was on the other side of the volcano, and Mama could not trust her sisters, Caterina, Ida, Rita, and Lucia, and her brothers, Guglielmo, Lorenzo, and Pietro, to protect her interests in the matter of *il testamento*.

Mama knew there was money hidden all over the house: in teapots and biscuit tins in the kitchen, in the mattress, the cellar, the eaves, and the wardrobe, and her nature was such that she could not stand idly by and permit herself and her brood to be robbed by her own siblings.

In addition to the money, there was the matter of the linen and furniture promised to her, the carpets and kitchenware, the clothes and the crockery, and some few remaining pieces of silver that had remained in her family since its descent from gentility in the Middle Ages to its present, more humble condition. Mama was proud of her family's heritage. Though Papa's family had land, Mama's had nothing to show for its lineage except a few relics of a former glory. Still, Mama liked it to be known that she had married down. She approached Nonna Calzino's deathbed with the intention to have it all, and what she could not get she would fight for nonetheless.

Mama drove off at a pace in the cart, taking the half-witted farmhand, Rosario, to protect her from the *banditti* then known to be lurking in the hills. As she left the farmyard Mama must have felt some strange misgiving, so she offered a prayer to the blessed Virgin, protector of the innocent, and urged her husband, Antonino Calabrese, to safeguard the virtue of her only daughter, Rosa, in her absence.

Catching a sly look passing over the features of the licentious Luigi, Mama fetched him a blow to the side of the head. The resounding smack was so powerful that it sent all lustful thoughts out of Luigi's mind, and they stayed away even after Mama was, by the grace of the holy Virgin, happily ensconced at home once more.

Nevertheless, as night fell Antonino Calabrese grew forgetful of his promise to safeguard my virtue and was tempted to take advantage of Mama's absence by bringing a barrel of grappa up from the cellar. He and his stepsons, my brothers Luigi, Leonardo, Mario, Giuliano, Giuseppe, and Salvatore, caroused in the kitchen while Guerra and Pace attended to their own concerns.

The twins were then nine and had for some years been running their own very successful business. From an early age they were thought to possess magical powers: clairvoyance, fortune-telling, and dowsing. The same villagers who had bayed for their blood at the time of their birth now consulted the twins as if they were oracles in the ancient tradition.

The lovelorn asked them how to engender desire in their chosen ones. Parents sought direction on how to deal with wayward children. Heirs sought counsel about undying benefactors. Wives consulted them on straying husbands.

The twins could tell a goatherd the precise whereabouts of a missing goat, or a farmer about the location of his mule, and predict the dates of births, deaths, plagues, and all other forms of disasters. They were able, with unerring accuracy, to predict the timing of an eruption of the volcano and the direction the lava flow would take, and for this valuable knowledge they charged a tidy sum.

Indeed they charged a high rate for all their services and were by nature incredibly parsimonious. During any free time when they were not giving consultations in the old pigsty that had been converted into an office, they would spend hours counting their gold, stroking it lovingly between their little fingers and smiling.

They had amassed a sizable fortune in their nine years, and as a sideline had begun to run a moneylending business. They made a fat profit on our own farmhands. On payday the workers would gather in the inn at Linguaglossa, where Luigi's sweetheart served behind the bar. There would be drinking contests and gambling and before the night was over their wages would all be spent. Then the twins would step in and supply the farmhands with sufficient cash to keep them until the next payday came, but at a rate which was never below 50 per cent.

Another of their ventures was to act as go-betweens between lovers, as they could be relied upon for their secrecy and discretion. They knew the business of everyone in the region, were feared and respected in equal measure, and because they spoke primarily in their own private language, some considered them to be on the edge of insanity.

When they reached puberty, the twins indulged their own precocious sexual development by siphoning off an amount from their profits to finance weekly visits to the whorehouse in Castiglione. This was where they met their future bride – but again I am racing ahead.

The twins acted as go-betweens for all of us in matters of the heart, myself included, but they charged members of their family the same rates as they did outsiders. After all, work was work, and they could not afford to be sentimental. The fact that I had been more of a mother to them than a sister did not entitle me to a discount.

And so the twins passed messages between me and my sweetheart, Bartolomeo, and however watchful Mama was, she never detected them.

CHAPTER EIGHT

And so, on the evening of Mama's departure for Adrano, I was able to slip away from the *fattoria* through the offices of Guerra and Pace to join Bartolomeo, and together we strolled through the meadows by the light of the winking stars.

The evening before, Bartolomeo had entrusted the twins with a message for me, saying that as a matter of greatest urgency I should meet him the next day at sunset. No matter how I wheedled and cajoled the twins, I could not prevail upon them to disclose to me the details of this urgent matter. Only when I gave them a silver coin did they reveal that Bartolomeo had kept his own counsel and not spoken of it, and as a matter of principle they would not use their clairvoyant powers to determine what it was.

I could scarcely contain my curiosity and I lay awake through the night inventing reasons to account for my absence, each less plausible than the last. The next morning I descended into the kitchen in complete despair, hoping that at least the preparation of some wild boar sausages would encourage my brain to think more creatively. Imagine my joy on discovering that Mama was to leave for Adrano immediately after *la colazione* and was to stay away overnight.

As the day passed I began to feel a deep excitement. I was filled with so much love for Bartolomeo that I feared I would burst if something did not happen soon. What that something was I did not know, for Mama kept me in a state of such complete innocence that at the age of seventeen I still did not know where babies came from, and thought that menstruation was the monthly consequence of eating too many artichokes.

As we strolled together, I could not help but feel a sense of triumph that I had outwitted Mama, who was at that precise moment arguing over feather beds with her sisters in Adrano; but I also remember feeling a sense of danger, knowing that I was crossing a boundary into the unknown. I felt happy but frightened to be there.

The two of us wandered together, our arms around each other's waists, through the olive groves and down into the valley beyond the confines of our farmland. Around us hung an aura of expectation that was almost tactile. Its heavy scent was familiar to the shepherd Luciano, whom we passed in the pasture tending his flock, and who, that night in bed, announced to his wife that Isabella Calabrese would pay a high price for her visit to Adrano in spite of the fine linen and cooking pots with which she would load her cart and return to Castiglione.

'So, Bartolomeo,' I asked, 'what is the very important thing that you must tell me?'

'Rosa, it is very important,' he replied in earnest. 'To-morrow I have to go away.'

'Go away?' I cried, my face falling like a collapsed soufflé.

'Yes, I must leave tonight. I shouldn't really be here now. I only stayed so I could see you before I go.'

'But why must you go? Where are you going?' I asked, my bottom lip protruding as tears began to gather in my eyes.

'I am going to take a steamship to the United States, Rosa, to Chicago, but you mustn't be sad, for I will send for you in a very short time. You will come to me and then we will be married.'

'Will we?' I asked, brightening momentarily but clouding again as I asked, 'But why are you going?'

'I have had a disagreement with my father and have to go away until it blows over. You know what he's like. Anyway, it is the best thing. We'll start a new life there. There's nothing for us here, just fields and olives and sheep. In the States there are big cities with tall buildings reaching right into the clouds and the people all drive automobiles and wear smart clothes and have pots of money. There are lots of opportunities for young people who are prepared to work hard. I will go to my mother's brother, Zio Genco, and he will help me. Then as soon as I can I will send for you. But you must be brave and patient and not tell anyone in case they try to stop us.'

'Oh, I won't tell anyone, Bartolomeo,' I said, setting in motion a procession of fantasies that included a mental snapshot of me on a cruise liner bound for the United States, then in a bridal gown dancing with Bartolomeo at our wedding. But then my thoughts turned to Mama's fury when she discovered that I had gone to America. I knew she planned to keep me at home to help on the farm and to wait on her as she grew older. She would be furious if her plans collapsed.

We reached the ruined castle of Conte Ruggero, its jagged outline framing the emerald sky. Here we had played as children, Bartolomeo the prince of the Arabs and I his mysterious eastern queen.

Bartolomeo led me inside and said, 'Rosa, there is something we have to do before I go, so that we will truly belong to one another and they can never separate us.'

Drawing me to him, he began to unlace my bodice. I let him. I did not really see why he shouldn't. Then his warm, moist kisses wandered from my mouth, across my cheeks to my earlobes. His tongue strayed inside my ears, probing, exploring, and the squelching this made, combined with the sound of his panting breath, made me feel feverish, confused, and unbearably happy all at the same time.

Bartolomeo's tongue strayed down to my throat and neck, biting it gently. Then, exposing my breasts, he took my nipples between his lips, one and then the other, kissing, sucking, and nibbling, until they hardened to resemble rosehips in their shape, size, and texture.

All the while he murmured to me in a voice as low and tender as the breeze with which it mingled, his words undulating, being carried aloft through the ruined turrets and then gradually dissipating, falling, and being lost for ever in all but my memory.

I remember feeling ecstasy and guilt in equal measure.

I wanted to run away and yet I wanted more. I felt a crackling electricity, its spark coursing the length of my torso and culminating in a throbbing ache in my loins, which I was too naive to understand and enjoy.

Bartolomeo pulled away my dress and long panties, leaving me naked in the moonlight and flushing hot to the roots of my hair with a searing embarrassment.

I shivered although I was not cold, and abandoned myself to the aching pains which made me want to cry out loud while my beloved removed his own clothes. I was completely shocked to see his penis standing erect and almost angry at an acute angle to his body.

It seemed a thing with an independent existence, and I was scared of its obscene magnificence. Although I had eight brothers, I had never seen such a sight, and I have to confess I was repulsed and fascinated by it.

Bartolomeo guided my hand towards it and I felt it clumsily, tentatively, not knowing what to do with it, and feeling quite afraid. It felt smooth, hard, cool, and unlike anything I had ever touched before. I must have done it reasonably well, for Bartolomeo gasped at my touch and pulled me down to the ground. He climbed on top of me and felt surprisingly heavy for such a slim boy. I could not really breathe but I did not want to say anything.

Suddenly I felt the most unexpected pain in the secret place between my legs. A searing pain that scorched through me like a hot poker. I didn't know what it meant then, but it was of course Bartolomeo forcing himself inside me.

I screamed out loud but he covered my mouth with his

so that now I could not breathe at all. I tried in vain to wriggle out from underneath him, to free myself from that brutal and persistent thing that was wrenching me apart and was surely going to kill me.

At the very point when I knew I was going to die, Bartolomeo gave one last enormous, wood-splitting thrust and then suddenly lay still, panting for breath, and pressing so heavily on my rib cage that I very nearly suffocated.

'I'm sorry it hurt you, Rosa,' said Bartolomeo when he had finally recovered his breath. 'It always hurts the first time. After that it gets much easier.'

Right then I was very sure there wasn't going to be a second time.

'Does it not hurt you, Bartolomeo?' I asked.

'Oh, no,' he replied. 'It gives me such a feeling of relief when I have discharged myself. All my troubles seem so little and I feel free as a bird flying over the sea or a feather floating downstream.'

I could not at all understand how this could be so, but my musings were interrupted by the discovery that the insides of my thighs were covered in blood.

'You have killed me, Bartolomeo,' I cried piteously, pointing to the bloodstains.

'No, Rosa, I haven't killed you. It is usual for a girl to bleed the first time. Surely you know that?'

'I know that I have not eaten an artichoke for a long time,' I said stiffly.

Bartolomeo smiled at me as though I were stupid, and as he dabbed me clean he said: 'Rosa, there are many things that I need to explain to you, things that your mother should have told you; I will tell them to you when we are together again.'

'Very well,' I replied, greatly relieved that I was not going to die, and clinging to Bartolomeo's neck I covered him with kisses.

CHAPTER NINE

'Father, forgive me, for I have sinned,' I said, crossing myself as I settled down on my knees in the confessional.

'What was your sin, my child?' asked Padre Francesco from behind the grille.

I paused before I answered, trying to frame my words. I felt a deep sense of shame and an awareness that the world had suddenly changed and would never be the same again. I was no longer the girl I had been yesterday; everything was imperceptibly yet definitely different.

It was very late when I had left Bartolomeo in the upper pastures. He had stayed too long. He should have left earlier, but it was so hard to part. Each time he set off on his long journey he turned and ran back again for one final kiss, then another, and another still. With tears filling my eyes I finally watched him disappear into the darkness and then I came through the gate into the farmyard and slipped quietly up the steps into *la cucina*.

I could not quite quell my feelings of unease, and even

the comfort of preparing a dish of *fritteɗɗa* could not calm me. Something was very wrong if my food could not comfort me.

I tiptoed to my room and splashed my face with water, and as I caught sight of my reflection in the looking glass over the washstand it seemed to me that my face had changed; I looked somehow older and not like my usual self. Removing my soiled clothes I could still smell Bartolomeo on my skin, a warm and delicious scent of fermenting sheep's yogurt, barley, and wood smoke which I did not want to wash away.

The smell emanating from between my legs was stronger still, musky and salty and pungent. I knew Mama's sharp nostrils would fix upon these alien scents immediately upon her entrance into *la cucina* the following morning, and so sadly I rubbed them away with my sponge, hiding my drawers with my other secret little treasures in the space under the loose floorboard so Mama would not notice their stench and watery blood-stains while sorting the laundry.

I lay down and tried to sleep, but I tossed and turned, and couldn't settle. In my mind I relived every moment of the past evening, and began to feel guilty about what had passed between us. I was scared of Mama's homecoming. I felt she would look at me with her black eyes and somehow know what had happened in her absence. Then there would be trouble, I knew.

As I turned over for the hundredth time I had the idea of going to confession. I knew it helped others in times of trouble, and I hoped that talking to the priest would soothe my soul the way a dish of *fritteɗɗa* usually did.

Once I had been given absolution for my sins perhaps I could meet Mama's inquisitional gaze without betraying myself.

Impatiently I watched it grow light and then made myself wait some more because it was still too early. Then, when life on the farm finally began to stir in the new day, I wrapped a shawl around my shoulders, for the air was still damp and cool, and hurried the few kilometres to *la chiesa*. Padre Francesco, the town's only priest, was still opening the doors and tending the altar when I asked him to hear my confession.

'I have sinned much, Father,' I said at last, summoning my courage.

'In what way, my child?' asked the priest.

'The sins of the flesh, Father,' I blurted out, after a long pause.

'Come now, explain it all to me, my child, and the good Lord will forgive you.'

'Well, Father, Mother went to Adrano because Nonna Calzino is dying . . .'

'May the Lord God grant her eternal peace,' interjected the priest, crossing himself.

'. . . Mama has gone to bring back what is rightly hers, what has been promised to her, and what Zia Caterina, Zia Ida, Zia Rita, and Zia Lucia, and Zio Guglielmo, Zio Lorenzo, and Zio Pietro have no right to . . .' I continued, reciting Mama's words, which I had heard many times, especially in recent days when the good Lord was preparing to draw Nonna Calzino to His holy side.

'Your mother is a dutiful daughter, Rosa,' sighed the priest, crossing himself once more.

'So, my child,' he went on, 'what has this to do with the sins of the flesh?'

'I sinned, Father,' I said. 'When Mama had gone to Adrano, Antonino Calabrese brought up the barrel of grappa from the cellar. Luigi, Leonardo, Mario, Giuliano, Giuseppe, and Salvatore helped him to drink the grappa. They sang songs and danced. The twins were attending to their business out in the pigsty.'

'And what did you do, my little Rosina?' asked the priest.

'I went walking in the pastures, Father.'

'Alone, child?'

'No, Father.'

'With whom did you walk in the pastures while your mother was away from home, Rosa?'

'With Bartolomeo, Father.'

'Bartolomeo Sogno?'

'Yes, Padre.'

'My poor, poor child,' murmured the priest. 'Go on.'

'We walked a long way, Father. Down through the valley to the old fairy castle, and there we did things.'

'What things, Rosa?'

'Things without our clothes on,' I said, hanging my head.

'I see,' said the priest sternly. 'You have sinned greatly, Rosa, very greatly, and for me to be able to tell how great the sin was I will need you to describe the things that you did in exact detail, the both of you, without your clothes on.'

Faltering, and burning with shame, I described in a

voice scarcely louder than a whisper the course of events
as they had taken place.

I noticed as my story unfolded that Padre Francesco's
breathing was becoming much heavier on the far side of
the grille. He began, it appeared to me, to twitch and to
jerk, and then he began to pant in that same strange way
that Bartolomeo had the night before while he was lying
on top of me. Then the *padre* began to groan, his moans
filling the chapel until, all of a sudden, at the climax of
my confession, they ceased.

'And so, Father,' I said, breaking in on the long pause
that followed. 'What is my absolution?'

'Your absolution, Rosa, is to come and make that same
confession tomorrow,' murmured the priest in a small
voice, 'and mind that you do not change a word of it, for
the Holy Father will know if you do and your sins will be
multiplied a hundredfold.'

'Thank you, Father,' I said as I crossed myself and left
the confessional, trying to feel cheerful, but in reality
feeling more uncomfortable and heavy with sin than I
had before.

Looking around, I noticed Nonna Sogno, Bartolomeo's
grandmother, sobbing violently in the Sogno family
pew. Strange. Again crossing myself, I left *la chiesa* and
emerged into the bright daylight of the piazza.

CHAPTER TEN

While Padre Francesco was attending to my confession, in a grey lava-stone town house on the far side of Randazzo, Donna Sophia Bacci lay with her face buried in the soft pillows of her heavy oak four-poster. Periodically her tiny frame, clothed in black, was convulsed by sobs, desperately gasping for breath. Then she would remain silent until the sobs welled up again and had to be released in a burst.

Sophia fixed her eyes on the white sunlight that forced its way through a small chink in the shutters, slicing through the solid darkness of the chamber and forming a burning brand on the ceiling.

A solitary fly made a rectangular motion in the centre of the room beneath the lantern. Again and again it traced the same pattern.

No one knew that Sophia had loved Bartolomeo since they had both attended the wedding of Sophia's cousin, Franco, when she was twelve years old. She remembered that day very clearly. She had watched Bartolomeo as he stood shyly in the corner of the churchyard while the photographs were being taken: bride and groom, bride and groom with bride's family, with groom's family, and finally the whole family of some three hundred people, two dogs, and a goat.

A dead lizard lay on the sand and Bartolomeo explored it with his toe as he waited for the grown-ups to finish talking. A succession of distant relatives ruffled his hair and pinched his cheeks.

I cannot say for certain what it was about Bartolomeo that marked him out as an object of such intense passion when he was a boy, but as Sophia watched him toying with the dead lizard she came to love him, and from that moment onward she loved him quietly but fully for the rest of her life.

Sophia had seen Bartolomeo occasionally at weddings and funerals and festivals but had never once spoken a word to him. Her diary entries of the period record her girlish ardour for the boy whose death she would eventually and unwittingly cause.

When, in her seventeenth year, her father, Don Fredo, proposed the match with Bartolomeo, it seemed to Sophia that her dreams had literally come true. The love she had nurtured in secret for so long was finally to bear fruit.

The night before the tragedy, as she prepared herself for the betrothal at the house of the Sogno, Sophia could not quite believe her good fortune. While performing her toilette she took time to unlock her little chest of treasures, the girlish relics of five years of yearning. The fork from which Bartolomeo had eaten at the wedding where she first saw him; the rose, withered and parched, which he had thrown with his own hand onto the grave during the funeral of Don Vito Barzini a year later; an olive stone which he had spat out at another wedding; a button from his shirt; a used paper napkin; and a single hair that she had removed surreptitiously from his coat collar at the Festival of Light the year before.

Sophia pored over her little treasures now with the same sense of awe that she had felt for them in the past, when Bartolomeo remained to her an impossible dream. Now she was to be his wife, and this very evening she was to see him, talk to him for the first time, if she was bold enough to find her voice, and possibly even receive a kiss from him.

Sophia felt faint at the very thought of all the happiness in store. She imagined herself in the church taking her wedding vows, Bartolomeo lifting her veil and gasping at her beauty. She imagined the wedding night, when he would remove her bridal gown and take her to him, blushing as a virgin should at the raucous innuendo of the serenading crowd gathered beneath the window. She imagined the birth of their first child, a boy whom she would name Bartolomeo after his father. Never would a child be so loved.

Sometimes it is better for our wishes not to be granted. Our dreams should remain dreams for our own good. Our prayers are only answered by a jealous God. When we get what we want most it is a sure sign that our troubles are about to begin in earnest.

Sophia's mother, Donna Theresa, smoothed her daughter's golden hair and applied cologne to her temples and her wrists. When little Sophia sobbed, Donna Theresa's pain showed itself in the puckering of her brow and the twitching of her lips. She wished she could ease her daughter's suffering, but she couldn't.

After a period of respite Sophia began to wail again, clutching herself and rocking backwards and forwards on the bed. Donna Theresa made a soft tutting noise, drawing her tongue down from behind her expensive teeth, and raised her eyes to the portrait of the Madonna hanging on the wall above the bed. The Madonna too cradled her child in her arms.

'Shush shush shush, my child,' murmured Donna Theresa in a soothing voice and rustling silk. 'Dry your tears. You know there could be no other way. Bartolomeo brought shame upon us and upon his own family. His father did the only thing he could do as a man of honour; and had he not done his duty, the deed would have fallen to your dear father and brothers. Do not forget that while we as fools were waiting at the house bearing gifts to consummate your betrothal, your precious Bartolomeo was lying in the arms of that coarse peasant girl. Surely knowing that, knowing that he rejected you for his wife, and scorned connection with your family, bringing dishonour upon us; knowing all of this, you cannot still find it in your heart to love him?'

'But I do, Mama,' choked Sophia, who was again convulsed by sobs.

CHAPTER ELEVEN

In the house of the Sogno, high in the steep streets of Castiglione, the body of Bartolomeo was laid out on the table in the front parlour, surrounded by spluttering candles and the heavy scent of lilies.

Crimson paper lined the walls, the colour of the inside of an eyelid. Little lace-fringed doilies, the handiwork of Bartolomeo's five sisters, protected the polished wooden sideboard from the scratches of the photograph frames arranged in clusters along its length.

Some of the photographs recorded special moments from Bartolomeo's childhood. In one he was a baby lying on a sheepskin rug in a photographer's studio in Randazzo. In another he was a child of five, carrying a new satchel for his first day at school. The most recent showed him as a handsome young man of seventeen. This was the photograph that was to adorn his grave.

The undertaker, Ernesto Tombi, clothed in black tail-coat and tight trousers, was plying his tape measure. A rich man from a long line of undertakers, he treated death like business; he could not afford to be sentimental.

With a flourish he took notes on a clipboard. Behind him a group of women, friends, neighbours, and passers-by gathered in the shadows. Some were gasping, some were weeping, some were outright screaming. In Sicily a murder is a public event, open to all.

On one side of the body sat Donna Evangelina Sogno, Bartolomeo's mother, who, with eyes as swollen as a toad's, held her son's cold hand and sporadically covered it with kisses.

On the other side of the table stood Don Umberto Sogno, the father and the murderer. He stood tall, his eyes were dry. He was a man of honour.

'Blessed Mary Mother of God!' cried Donna Evangelina. 'How could we have come to this: a son murdered by his father's hand!' She succumbed to a wrenching sobbing, tearing at her hair and rocking herself back and forth in her chair.

'My son. My son!' she screamed, gasping for breath. Her five daughters, Ginevra, Perla, Margarita, Lucia, and Anna, held their mother up to prevent her from fainting while taking turns at screaming and swooning.

'Enough, woman,' said Don Umberto in a quiet voice edged with steel. 'Your son had no respect; he chose to disobey me; he is no longer *my* son. Once the burial has taken place his name will be heard no more in this house.'

'May the Lord God forgive you for those words, Don Umberto,' said Padre Francesco loudly to announce his presence.

'It is more than words He will need to forgive, Father,' sobbed Donna Evangelina.

'He!' she screamed pointing at her husband. 'He has killed my son, my only son, my Bartolomeo. A father who kills his own son. Evil, evil man. Monster.'

At this Donna Evangelina collapsed, hitting her head on the floor, and was carried out of the room by her daughters. In the hubbub that followed some of the candles were knocked over, causing a small fire to break out, while a thief who had entered the house with the crowd of mourners seized the opportunity to fill his pockets with silver and other valuable goods.

'Is it true that you are responsible for the boy's death, Don Umberto?' whispered the priest.

'Remember who secured your release from prison, *Padre*,' whispered Don Umberto with a sneer. 'Do not forget who arranged for your new identity and a comfortable living. Imagine how shocked many of your lady parishioners would be to discover your true story. I would advise you not to vex me with any of your questions.'

Padre Francesco wisely noted Don Umberto's advice and slunk away.

Next, Donna Rubino Sogno, Don Umberto's mother arrived at the house. All of Castiglione feared Don Umberto. Don Umberto feared his mother. Nonna Sogno was small but fierce; she was the size of a half-grown child, but a child with grey hair and no teeth.

When she came in, the crowd of mourners retreated to give her passage.

'Get out of here, you useless bunch of hangers-on,' she said through her boneless gums.

The crowd evaporated, leaving the parlour empty

except for the corpse of Bartolomeo, Don Umberto, and Donna Rubino.

Donna Rubino approached the corpse. She kissed Bartolomeo gently on the forehead, and made the sign of the cross while muttering her prayers. A tear traced its path down her withered cheek and plopped onto her bodice, where it glistened for a while before sinking into the cloth.

She turned to her son, Don Umberto, whose pretence of self-assurance was betrayed by a slight shiver of fear. Donna Rubino spat and the bullet of saliva hit her son square in the eye, blinding him temporarily.

'I curse you with a mother's curse,' she whispered in a voice that made the hairs on the back of Don Umberto's neck and forearms rise like the hackles of a frightened hound.

'You scum,' she said quietly. 'You whore. You have killed my grandson, your own son, with your own hand. Through the will of the Holy Virgin I discover I have borne a monster in my womb. Now I place my curse upon you. My curse will follow you always. Never will you be free of it. By day it will be there. You will wake in the night to see it sitting at the foot of your bed. It will never cease in its pursuit of you. You will be constantly looking over your shoulder. You will die with all the agony of a thousand deaths. Bartolomeo will be avenged on you for this.'

After she finished, Donna Rubino spat again with unerring accuracy, and hit Don Umberto squarely in the other eye. Then she turned majestically on her diminutive heel and left the house of her son for the last time.

Don Umberto wiped his eyes. For the first time he doubted his righteousness.

Were his wife and mother right? Was he really a monster to kill his own child, the fruit of his loins? Or was he a reasonable man, protecting his honour in the only way possible?

If another man had disobeyed him, would he hesitate to have him cut down like a dog? Did his son owe him not less, but even more obedience than someone outside the family? Was his son's crime not the more heinous for that? Did he not therefore deserve to die? Surely Don Umberto was acting with honour in killing the boy himself, instead of passing out the instruction to one of his henchmen. Surely this in itself was the act of a loving father?

Don Umberto's head pulsed with the pressure of his thoughts. A sweat bead stood on his brow.

Was he right or was he wrong?

Cursed by his mother, shunned by his wife and daughters, he knew he would not find comfort in the home.

Should he go to church? Ask for God's guidance and deliverance? He rose to do so, but then slumped down again into his chair, for he was not a believer, and, besides, the bogus priest could not help him find God.

A commotion outside interrupted Don Umberto's brooding.

It was me, Rosa, bursting into the room.

On seeing the body laid out on the table I approached it slowly and carefully, staring at it silently. It was as though my mind had gone. I stroked Bartolomeo's face with my fingertips, mumbling to myself incomprehensible words; then I pulled the bandage away from his throat and saw the neat incision marked with a fine line of dried blood. Then I started to scream hysterically and uncontrollably until Don Umberto silenced me with a resounding slap across the face.

'Leave this house,' he hissed. 'You whore, you caused all this. Had it not been for you my son would not have betrayed me; it is you, not I, who bears his blood upon your hands and you will do so until the day you die. My curse will be upon you until your final breath. Now get out of my house!'

He threw me from the front steps into the street, where I was almost mown down by the passing traffic. I was covered in muck and dust. I could not rise up by myself, and no-one would help me. It was a while before Guerra and Pace made their way through the crowd and helped me to stumble away.

CHAPTER TWELVE

I could not really remember a time when I had not known Bartolomeo. We met at the *scuola elementare* in the class of Sister Pazienza. Back then, educating girls was regarded as a waste of money, but Mama insisted on sending me despite Papa's objections. I was five and the only girl at the school. Bartolomeo and I sat at adjoining desks and pretty soon we became the best of friends.

From that first day we were always together. We shared our lunches in the schoolyard, under the shade of the big plane tree. I would give Bartolomeo half my pie or cheese. He often had sweets or a chocolate bar, and would carefully divide them between us. Sometimes he had gum, which was a treat in those days, and we would take turns at chewing it. After the long days in the classroom Bartolomeo walked me home through the fields of poppies, carrying my satchel.

When I was about thirteen we started to hold hands, and, when no-one else was around, we exchanged innocent kisses.

Nothing went unnoticed by Mama, and she strongly

disapproved of our juvenile courtship. She disapproved because of Bartolomeo's birthright. He was of the Sogno, and as everyone in the region knew, the Sogno were men of honour. That is, they were *la famiglia*, the Mafia.

Mama, like many others, had lived in fear of the Mafia all her life. The tales she heard at her mother's knee were of the murderous exploits of the men of honour, and with Mama, who took everything literally, myth had fused with reality. Had Bartolomeo been part of another family, Mama would have paid a visit to his parents and ordered them to keep their son away from her daughter. But in this case, Mama, who was so used to exercising control, was afraid and powerless.

All Mama could do was to warn me of the dangers, and of course I paid no heed. Bartolomeo showed no signs of being like his father; he was a gentle boy, courteous and kind. But Mama, trusting no-one, was convinced that his gentle manner was a convenient cover for a violent and evil-tempered nature. As far as she was concerned, Bartolomeo was capable of blackmail, extortion, and even murder.

Mama had lived through many vendettas, some of which had left families in the region without a single son to carry on their names. She feared for her Rosa keeping such company, and did all she could to discourage our intimacy.

Donna Evangelina Sogno knew with a mother's intuition of her son's affection for me. She also knew that her husband was planning an advantageous match for Bartolomeo when he reached twenty-one. She knew Don Umberto wanted to marry him off to Donna Sophia

Bacci in order to cement an alliance with her father, Don Fredo Bacci, another patrician of the eastern branch of *la famiglia*.

Donna Evangelina also knew her husband would not be dissuaded from his goal by the simple fact that his son was in love with another girl, and a peasant at that. She knew her husband's steely determination to do things his own way, and his terrible temper if ever his will was challenged.

If Bartolomeo had inherited anything from his father it was his obduracy and strength of will. Donna Evangelina had every reason to fear the consequences of the inevitable conflict between father and son, and she prayed to the Virgin for intercession.

One evening Don Umberto Sogno was unusually cheerful. He had concluded a deal that would place every road-building contract in the east of the island under his control. This deal had been subject to long and careful negotiations, and today the final obstacle represented by the mulish Don Michele Caciocavallo had been removed by the skilful positioning of a bomb outside his house.

Don Umberto, mellow with success and grappa in equal measure, gathered his family around him in the parlour: his wife, Donna Evangelina, and his five daughters, Ginevra, Perla, Margarita, Lucia, and Anna. He called Bartolomeo to his side and embraced him, kissing him on both cheeks. Resting his arm around Bartolomeo's shoulders, he turned to his wife and daughters and said: 'My dears, I have good news for you. My son, my only son, Bartolomeo, is to be married.'

Donna Evangelina and her daughters, aware of the heartbreak this would cause, all blanched. Only Bartolomeo retained his composure.

Don Umberto slapped Bartolomeo on the back, smiling broadly. 'Well, what is the matter with you all? Are none of you curious about the bride? I will tell you. She is Donna Sophia Bacci, daughter of my esteemed friend Don Fredo Bacci. It is a good match, a fine connection between our families, for it will cement our allegiance with another ancient branch of *la famiglia*. Tomorrow, in the evening, the Bacci family will come here to celebrate the betrothal. Wife, put out the best wine and food that we have. We will entertain our in-laws royally.'

Don Umberto was then called away to attend to business. He left his family in a stunned silence.

'What will you do, my son?' asked Donna Evangelina as soon as her husband had left the room.

'I will not do it, Mama. I cannot. I cannot marry this girl.'

'But Bartolomeo, you have no choice. Your father has expressed his will. You cannot disobey him. You know that.'

'I must, Mama. I cannot marry someone I do not love. It would bring misery to this girl, to myself, and to others.' He stopped to think for a moment.

'I will go away somewhere. Yes, I will go to Zio Genco in Chicago, he will help me, and you must explain it to Papa for me after I'm gone. You must find me the money for the passage, and pack me a few things in a bag. I will set off tomorrow, after dark.'

'But what about tomorrow night, Bartolomeo, when the Baccis are coming?'

'Do as Papa says, Mama. Prepare everything according to his wishes. Do not let your behaviour reveal to him that anything is wrong. While you are entertaining them here I will make my escape.'

And so Bartolomeo went off to send his message to me via the twins, while his mother and sisters began, with heavy hearts, the preparations in celebration of the betrothal that would never take place.

CHAPTER THIRTEEN

The evening of celebration had begun on a cheerful note. The best wine was served in the crystal goblets, and the girls took turns demonstrating their talents on the piano.

The fathers, seated in the high-backed armchairs by the window, talked business in an undertone, drank grappa, and smoked cigars. The mothers swapped anecdotes about their offspring and leafed through the many photograph albums. Around the piano the Bacci boys flirted with the Sogno girls. Donna Sophia watched the door for the arrival of her beloved. Having waited so long for this moment, she was growing impatient now.

In time the hot snacks cooled and dried up, and Bartolomeo had yet to appear. The smiles became more laboured, the conversation grew increasingly tense and awkward.

Donna Evangelina became more and more anxious, and at every sound assured everyone gathered that Bartolomeo had finally arrived, although in her heart she hoped her son was by now miles away.

Finally, after more than two hours had passed, Signor

Bacci drew himself up to his full height, which was not much greater than that of a mule, and, nodding slightly to his wife, sons, and by now his sobbing daughter, left the house in anger.

Don Umberto followed Don Fredo into the courtyard, and while the *signora* and her offspring arranged themselves in the carriage, Don Umberto murmured, 'Believe me, Don Fredo, Bartolomeo will pay the price of the dishonour he has brought to your house and to mine.'

'That I do not doubt, Don Umberto,' replied Don Fredo quietly. 'For if his father does not advise him of his error in judgement, my sons will supply the necessary instruction.'

With that Don Fredo mounted into the carriage, which quickly disappeared over the flagstones into the silence of the town now preparing for slumber.

Silence enveloped the house of Sogno. Donna Evangelina and her daughters wept quietly in their rooms while Don Umberto waited for news. He paced up and down the parlour, which only hours before had seemed so full and festive. In his hand he held a knife, and he tested the sharpness of its blade on his thumb.

At last a shadowy figure came to the door, interrupting the eerie sound of Don Umberto's regular steps. It was one of his henchmen, Barese.

'He has been found, Don Umberto,' Barese whispered. 'He was with that girl of Fiore's. Now he's heading in the direction of the piazza. Pirone is tailing him. He may try and get the late bus out of town. Do you want me to deal with him?'

Don Umberto narrowed his eyes and held up his knife

to indicate that he himself would do the deed. They left the house together, silently drawing the door to a close behind them.

Don Umberto and his accomplice walked briskly across town to the Piazza di San Antonio, and hiding in the shadows near the bus stop they waited for Bartolomeo to appear. The grumbling engine of the approaching bus was the only sound. It was driven by one of Barese's thousand cousins. When the time came he would see nothing. Word had gone around, and there were no other passengers waiting to board the bus. No one in Castiglione wanted to risk upsetting Don Umberto. Those who had a journey to make would postpone their departure until tomorrow.

Suddenly Bartolomeo came into view, running lightly from the direction of the Piazza Laura. As he ran he looked around in all directions, scanning the shadows for signs of danger. He knew his father would be after him, and his father's henchmen. But there didn't appear to be anyone following him. He had to get away quickly before they found him. He had meant to make his escape earlier, while his father was still entertaining the Baccis. But time had somehow slipped away and now he was late. He hoped he wasn't too late.

Bartolomeo could already see the bus. It was running on time. He was nearly there. All he had to do was get on it, get out of Castiglione and away to safety: to the mainland, and from there to Chicago.

The doors of the bus were open. He was about to climb the steps. He had made it. But then his father stepped out of the shadows. Bartolomeo received no warning. Only the silent anger of his father's face, the glint of a blade, before his eyes filled with a blinding tide of blood.

The body fell to the ground; the blood pumping from the wound stained the flagstones of the piazza. The bus driver closed the doors and drove off as if he had seen nothing.

La Primavera

THE SPRING

CHAPTER ONE

It was a day in April in the year 1958. A day of squally showers, of fat slippery drops that slither their way between the back of the neck and the collar of the raincoat.

As the umbrellas went up in a sudden flowering, the sun came out, and we were glad. The pigeons flapped and scratched and cooed; there were shiny puddles on the pavement; dogs sniffed the freshly washed scents. Pink powder puffs hung from the trees; wind blew.

Poor bedraggled Rosa. The umbrella always seemed to blow itself inside out. It was difficult to carry the packages from the market and the umbrella at the same time. I kept juggling. I wouldn't allow myself to drop the fresh eggs, no. Or the green cauliflower, ripe yet firm. The delicate rose-coloured tuna wrapped in paper; silky skin, so tender to the touch.

It was essential to get to market early, before work, while everything was fresh, before it had been picked over and pawed by housewives. I loved my daily visits to the market, seeing all of nature's bounty beautifully arranged for me to choose from. The aroma of the fresh peas, mint, and basil mingled with the smell of raw meat hanging at the butcher's and reminded me of my early life on the farm.

It had been only two years since the food riots in the city, when gang warfare among the rival clans of the Mafia stopped supplies of fresh produce from getting through. Shortages and terrible queues marked our daily lives and I often found myself coming to blows with a rival over a skinned rabbit or a bunch of carrots. Those were dark days indeed.

The bells of San Domenico chimed a quarter to nine. I would have to rush. I could not be late. No. I had never once been late. Not in twenty-five years. I rushed. A gush of icy water sloshed into my shoe. Now I'd be wearing wet stockings all day.

I struggled to open the door while grasping my packages. I closed the umbrella and placed it in a stand with its dripping friends.

'*Buongiorno*, Crocifisso,' I said to the doorman, who was reading the headlines of *Il Giornale*: MAFIA – NEW RACKET UNCOVERED.

'*Buongiorno*, Signorina Rosa. *Che tempo!*'

'*Si*, Crocifisso. *C'e la primavera.*'

I started work on the ledgers. There was so much work to do. I was interrupted almost immediately by Costanza.

'*Scusi*, Signorina Rosa,' she said.

'Yes?'

'There is a foreigner at the counter, signorina.'

'So?'

'He wants to look at the manuscripts.'

'But it's Tuesday, Costanza.'

'I have told him that, signorina. But he's a foreigner.'

'So?' again.

'He says again and again, signorina. He won't listen. He says "I see the manuscripts now." '

'Very well, Costanza. I will deal with him,' I said. 'But he must wait. I must finish this first.'

I continued to enter figures in my ledger as the insouciant Costanza teetered away in her tarty high heels, tip-tapping her way up the spiral staircase that led from the basement to the upper floors.

An hour later, when I had gathered together my papers, ledgers, ruler, sharpened pencils, and india rubber, I knew I had to turn my attention to the foreigner. I had never been able to leave a task half done.

CHAPTER TWO

I looked into the eyes of the foreigner. They were the colour of the sea off Taormina, more turquoise than blue and sparkling like the reflection of sunlight on water. They were the most mischievous eyes I had ever seen. I knew then I would have to be careful.

I remember he had a little moustache covering his upper lip; when he spoke, he revealed bad teeth. His nose was prominent, his hair fine and brown and thinning a little. I imagined the silkiness of his hair gently sweeping the contours of my bare flesh, the length of my spine, the valley between my breasts. Could this possibly be a premonition? I shivered.

He was wearing a cool linen suit and expensive brown brogues, smooth and shiny like melting ice cream. He smelled delicious, a mixture of fine eau de cologne and brandy. Something inside me heaved.

He took me in immediately with one deliberately slow and encompassing glance. He knew women and instinctively categorized them into types. He told me afterwards how my dowdy exterior could not hide from him my deeply sensuous nature. A little dry, perhaps, like a riverbed in summer, but not irredeemably so.

'Good morning, signorina,' he said in flawless Italian marked by an English accent. 'I am told you are the keeper of the manuscripts.'

'Yes, signor.'

'Let me introduce myself, I am Randolph Hunt. I am a scholar, signorina, and I am writing a book about the styles of cooking in the different regions of your beautiful island. I am currently researching how the Greeks, the Phoenicians, the Romans, the Arabs, the Normans, and the Spaniards influenced Sicilian cooking. I understand that you hold here in your archives the ancient manuscripts of Mithaecus, Archestratus, Dionysius, and others which trace the history of the island's cooking since the fifth century before Christ.'

'Yes, signor. The Biblioteca Nationale is proud to possess all of these works, and even more. It is a very rare and precious collection.'

'May I see them, signorina? They would be very valuable to my work.'

'Do you have a permit?'

'A permit?'

'Yes, signor. A permit from the Department of Cultural History.'

'I was told nothing about any permit, signorina.'

'If you do not have the necessary permit, signor, I am afraid I cannot help you,' I said, turning and preparing to descend the stairs into the basement.

'How do I acquire this permit, signorina?'

'You apply to the ministry, signor. Good day.'

'Good day, signorina. Many thanks for your kind assistance.'

L'Inglese took one final look at me, which made me break out in one of my sweats, and then turned to go. Before he reached the revolving door at the entrance, he abruptly turned around and came back again.

'Signorina?'

'Yes, signor?'

'You can't imagine how much I desire to make love to you at this moment.'

Aflame, I scuttled down the spiral staircase into the basement, pursued by Costanza's laughter. In no time at all she was telling her colleagues, the doorman, the university students, the regular readers, and even the postman and the milkman about the scandalous interchange, suitably embellished, between Signorina Fiore and the shameless foreigner.

That night I found it difficult to sleep, which was, for me, most unusual. At three I was in my little kitchen preparing a dish of *formaggio all' Argentiera*.

I fried slices of caciocavallo cheese with garlic until it had just melted and then sprinkled this with wine vinegar and fresh oregano before piling it onto a thick slice of rustic bread. The whole apartment block woke up to the sumptuous aroma of melted cheese and garlic escaping from my kitchen. Infants cried in imaginary hunger, dogs howled, husbands demanded that wives prepare a similar dish or threatened to make their way to my door. In response, the wives cursed me and my culinary arts and demanded to be allowed to get some sleep.

My parrot, Celeste, was most upset by this untimely

commotion, and she voiced her discontent with a series of muffled squawks, screams, and scratchings that I could hear beyond the cover of her cage.

The squinting grocer and her husband, both of them over a hundred years old, were not awoken by this cacophony, because mercifully they were not asleep. For the last eighty years it had been their practice to make love on a Tuesday evening, and this Tuesday evening was no exception.

As she deposited her teeth in the glass next to her husband's Nonna Frolla said: 'You can be sure, *bello*, our Rosa has something on her mind, for not once in the twenty-five years since she first moved in has she ever felt the need to prepare a dish of *formaggio all' Argentiera* at three o'clock in the morning.'

Before she fell into a sweet orgasmic sleep, the good lady made a mental note to find out the nature of my troubles first thing in the morning.

Yet even the cooking could not release my tension. I returned to bed but again tossed and turned, re-enacting for the fiftieth time the scene between myself and l'Inglese. The hot blush would not leave my cheeks. I burned with a fever that could not be quelled, even by the opening of a window on a cool April night.

When I finally fell asleep at dawn I was plagued by curious dreams from which I woke up sweating, parched, and panting.

In the first dream I was shopping in the market before work as usual, only I was totally naked and exposed in all my fulsome glory to the lewd remarks of the merchants and the titters of the housewives. In vain I tried to shield myself with my shopping basket, as I ran from the Piazza San Domenico down the Via Bandiera.

The cobbles cut into my feet with every step and my largesse wobbled and flapped.

At the end of the Via Bandiera stood a figure. As I came closer, panting and stumbling, I saw that it was l'Inglese. He had me fixed with those penetrating eyes, and however hard I tried I could not raise my bare feet from the cobbles where they were rooted. I stood frozen as a statue as l'Inglese approached me. He came so close I could smell him: the underlying but overpowering odour of a man.

L'Inglese stopped just short of touching my breasts with his body. He was so close that the air filling the tiny space where I ended and he began became highly charged with spikes and crackles and barbs.

I remember fighting through the smothering layers of sleep to wake myself from this nightmare, like a mummy trying to escape from its bandages. When I finally jerked my eyes open, imagine my horror at finding l'Inglese at the foot of the bed, standing casually and quite naked.

The scream dried in my throat. Silence filled this room-sized world. L'Inglese sniffed, in that aristocratic way he had, and the curl of his upper lip revealed the glint of the yellow teeth in the half-darkness.

He lifted the covers at the foot of the bed and burrowed underneath them. Suddenly the bed stretched and became the length of the street outside, and I watched the bulge that was l'Inglese as it inched closer and closer under the covers.

It came slowly but steadily, without stopping, along the centre of the bed, the glossy coverlet rising and falling.

My eyes followed it as it came on and on. I almost wanted it to come so that the agony of fear and suspense would be over.

Still it came, slowly and surely, and all I could do was wait for it. I had to force myself to breathe.

Finally it reached my feet. A mouth, it had to be a mouth, moist and warm, closed over one of my toes and started to suck it. Something resembling the bolt from a crossbow shot through the veins of my leg and exploded into a shower of shooting stars in the long-slumbering layers of my loins.

The mouth moved on and played in the spaces between my toes, where there are no toes, only tender spaces, and then it moved on to the other toes.

Now a tongue flickered on the soles of my feet, alternating between the left one and the right, while I writhed at the tickling and tried in vain to wriggle away.

Now hands had taken hold of me. Hands cool and dry. Small and manicured.

They stroked my feet in a rhythmic motion, and then moved on, up past my ankles to my calves, with so light a touch that I could not but purr like a massive cat.

The hands caressed my knees, and moved on again upward to my inner thighs, pushing back my nightgown and parting my legs. I gasped. The hands stroked my thighs like a whisper, as light as zabaglione.

The fingers then began their work. I could feel the pad of the fingertip applied squarely just with a hint of the tip of the nail, tracing a path up and down, up and down, the insides of my thighs. By now I had lost even the desire to resist. My longing was only that this torture never end.

The gentle fingers now strayed to the secret place between my legs, parting the silky hair and stroking the folds of flesh. My groans grew louder and louder, the faster and deeper and heavier the magic fingers probed and pressed and vibrated. The groans grew and grew in volume and strength until they filled the apartment block, wakening the residents for the second time that night.

There came a ferocious rapping at the front door, which entered the wonderful dream and tore me most unwillingly from it.

The parrot responded to the knocking with a perfect imitation of a dog's bark.

At the door was Nonna Frolla, the diminutive grocer, wearing nothing but a nightgown. Her arms were folded across her withered chest and her one good eye was flashing.

'Now, Rosa,' said her gums, for she had not had time to replace her teeth, 'in the name of the blessed Virgin, protector of the sleeping innocents, what is going on in here tonight?'

Once back in bed I tried in vain to re-enter the dream, but despite my best efforts it had gone.

CHAPTER THREE

The next day, I was again at work in the basement. After my hectic night, the first in twenty-five years, I was not in a happy mood, and my dissatisfaction was increased by my shame at never being able to look my neighbours in the face again.

I was roused from gloomy thoughts by Costanza, who summoned me to the front desk. L'Inglese was back, this time equipped with a permit.

When I had completed my cataloguing duties, I approached the counter on which l'Inglese was lolling, flirting ostentatiously with Costanza and the other airheads the director had seen fit to employ despite my reservations about their suitability for library work.

As his eyes turned towards me I flushed the deepest shade of red, fearing he could read from my eyes the substance of my dreams of the night before, which, to a greater or a lesser degree, he could do with just a glance. He knew I had not been able to stop thinking about him. He could tell. He had planned it that way.

'Good morning, signorina,' he said, reaching for my

hand and kissing the inside of my wrist. His moustache tickled the soft skin. I flushed again and drew my hand away. L'Inglese kept hold of one of my fingers, which he continued to caress as he spoke.

'Signorina, I have my permit,' he said, producing it with a flourish from his breast pocket.

I inspected it.

'So I see, signor,' handing it back.

'Is all now in order?' he asked.

'It appears to be.'

'So lead on, signorina, lead me to your basement where you hide yourself away. Lead me to your lair, and to your precious manuscripts.'

'I am afraid, signor, that that is impossible.'

'Impossible?'

'Impossible.'

'No, that cannot be. Why is it impossible?'

'It is impossible, signor, because today is Wednesday.'

'So?'

'So, the manuscripts may only be seen on Mondays.'

'I cannot believe it. I am a famous chef and author of books. I am involved in a very important piece of work. I ask to see the manuscripts. I am told I require a permit. I duly obtain the permit. Then I am told that I can only examine the manuscripts on a Monday. Today is Wednesday. I must kick my heels until Monday. That is five whole days – wasted. Wasted because of your petty bureaucracy. It is too much. Too, too much.'

'Those, signor, are the rules,' I said, turning to go.

'Signorina, signorina.' L'Inglese softened, his manu-factured rage subsiding immediately as he realized it would have no effect upon me. He prepared instead to try a different tactic.

'Let us be friends, eh?' he said. 'Let us co-operate with one another,' looking me directly in the eye, 'let us help one another, hmmmm?' edging very close.

'Monday, signor, come back on Monday.'

'Oh, signorina,' said l'Inglese, beaten, as I walked away, 'you drive me to distraction, you tantalizing woman.'

My heart was pounding as I retreated, forcing myself to retain the outward appearance of a composure I could barely sustain. I must not let him see that he had got to me, I knew that. I had no idea, however, that I might have got to him. I had no sense of the painfully cramped erection that was, at that very moment, straining inside his trousers as a result of this interchange; and indeed, he did not understand it himself. I was clearly not his type. The easy little tart at the front desk was probably more to his liking. But, as he said much later, there was definitely something about me. He thought I was a real woman, someone with courage and passion, a woman who was hiding from herself, but a woman who, once released from her self-imposed exile, would overwhelm him with the sheer exuberance of her return to life.

I only just made it to the ladies' room before my legs gave way beneath me and I slumped into the decaying sofa donated many years before by the director's wife.

I had a sudden fantasy of myself bending over the back of this very sofa with l'Inglese entering me from behind. I imagined the brief glorious instant of penetration and moaned out loud. Then I thought of his repeated thrusts, each deeper and more furious than the last, plumbing my innermost depths, and I almost heard the slap of his thighs against my bottom, before we reached in perfect unison a crescendo of agonizing orgasms.

It was some time later that Costanza found me straddling the back of the sofa. I must have passed out. I didn't have time for breakfast. Low blood sugar, that was all. Of course, no-one believed me. Costanza made sure that they didn't.

The university students and the regular readers eagerly anticipated the next instalment. It was, after all, far more interesting than the textbooks, the dusty periodicals, and yesterday's thumbed copy of *L'Ora*.

The day dragged on. All I wanted was to retreat inside my little apartment on the Via Vicolo Brugno and bolt the door behind me.

It was, however, not to be. Donna Maria Frolla was watching out for me as I walked up the steps, and followed me inside scrutinizing me closely with her one good eye. Her pug, Nero, gave me an arch look: his sleep too had been disturbed.

'It's a man, Rosa, isn't it?' she said with authority. 'I knew it had to be a man. I said last night to Papa, "It's a man. It would have to be a man to make our Rosa take on like this." Signora Prezzo came in to the shop this morning for her coffee – one hundred grams of finest blend – as usual – and she said to me, "Signora Frolla, there's a man in the case – there has to be," and of course she's right. Although to be sure Quinto Cavallo, the goldsmith from number seven, him with the workshop in the Via d'Oro – one hundred grams ricotta, one hundred

grams prosciutto, one cioccolata grande, one pane –
regular as clockwork on a weekday morning around eight
– he pointed out that it could be The Change. A similar
thing happened to an aunt of his over somewhere in the
west, in Trapani or Marsala. Or was it a cousin? Was it
out east? Anyway, when her turn came she carried on
something terrible. Up all night. Couldn't sleep. Banging
and crashing about in the kitchen, making enough noise
to raise the dead. Strange dreams. Feverish looks. "It's
the menopause," he said, "I'm prepared to put money on
it." I said to Papa, "It's hormones of one kind or another,
to be sure" . . .'

'Nonna Frolla, please . . .' I interrupted, burying my
head in my hands in shame.

'There's no "please" about it,' went on the centenarian
in full flow. 'You've lodged with me for twenty-five years.
Came here a slip of a girl, green as grass, to the big city. I
had my doubts on seeing you standing on the other side
of my counter with your little bag and your parrot—'

'Pretty parrot, pretty parrot,' chimed in Celeste, recog-
nizing her presence in the conversation.

'. . . wanting my rooms. Still, I took you for all that,
and never have I had a moment's trouble with you. That
is, until last night. First, there's the small matter of
a *formaggio all' Argentiera* being prepared in this very
kitchen at three o'clock this morning. Fortunately it
didn't wake Papa and me.' A glint appeared at this point
in her one good eye.

'But nevertheless, I've had complaints from the
tenants. Caused all sorts of trouble it has. Then, after
that, there was the noise. The queerest groans and gasps,

shrieks and screams, loud enough to raise the entire neighbourhood from its slumbers; not becoming in a single woman. Then the parrot joins in.'

'Parrot, parrot, parrot,' squawked Celeste.

'Enough noise to raise the dead. And when I roused you there was no explanation offered for it. Now, my girl, I need to know what is going on. Is there a man in it, or is it something else?'

'There isn't a man, Nonna,' I said, looking away.

'Then what is it?'

'Oh, I don't know. I don't know what it is. I just haven't been myself lately. Working too hard, I suppose . . .'

'Well, whatever it is it will have to stop, I tell you that now, upsetting the tenants, I can't have it, Rosa, I tell you, I just can't.'

CHAPTER FOUR

Nonna chattered on for a long time, prying and speculating on the cause of my malaise. When she finally left I sat at the open window, looking out on the darkened city illuminated by twinkling lights.

He was out there somewhere. Under that same moon, those same stars. I could almost feel him. Why was he having this effect on me? I had asked myself a thousand times. I had finished with foolish thoughts of love many years ago. I had crushed my heart like a clove of garlic in a mortar, crushed it into a dry powder that had simply drained away as sand through an hourglass, like the years of my youth, until there was nothing left. Or so I thought. What was now deep within me, stirring at my very core like the branches of the spring trees bursting overnight into fresh pink petals?

What was it about this Inglese that so affected me? I had only seen him twice, and then only briefly. He was not attractive, at least not in a conventional sense, and even if he were, I was immune to such things. I was not in love with him. That was not possible. I was incapable

109

of love. Perhaps it had no connection to him at all. Perhaps the feeling of longing was merely coincidental with his appearance at the library.

Where was he now?

What was he doing?

If I went out into the streets now would I meet him strolling along in his come-to-bed shoes?

He was probably out with someone else. Someone like that hussy Costanza – someone skinny with a shrieking laugh and too much lipstick.

What would he do until Monday?

Where would he go?

Should I have allowed him to see the manuscripts before Monday?

No, I could not have done that. He would have to wait like everyone else. Can you imagine the gossip if I had allowed him special privileges? No, I had done the right thing, even though he called me a petty bureaucrat, thinking I was an embittered old maid enjoying my little bit of power. But it wasn't like that. Those are the rules.

Today he said I drove him to distraction. He said I was a tantalizing woman. Was I really like that? Could I really be a temptress?

I suddenly had an impulse to see myself naked. I had only been naked in front of another person once, Bartolomeo, all those years ago. I was much younger then and my body was better. Also, it had been dark.

Suppose l'Inglese saw me naked. What would he think? Something told me he was the kind of man who would insist on having the lights on. I've read in women's magazines that many men are like that. I blushed at the mere idea.

How would it be if he removed my clothes? Could I really allow it? Quickly I removed my cardigan and sensible shoes. Then I unbuttoned my dress and, by wiggling my shoulders, let it slip down around me and onto the floor.

Emboldened, I turned on the radiogram. 'O la va, o la spacca!' was playing and I smooched around the apartment in time to the music. As I danced I caught sight of myself in the full-length mirror. Framed by the rectangle of light thrown by the lamp in the hall, I saw my upper arms were white and spongy. I turned sideways and looked at my profile, taking care to stand up straight and breathe in.

Then I pulled my slip up and over my head, began to fold it, and then, remembering that I was trying to be seductive, twirled it around and threw it over my shoulder.

Underneath, my corset was grey with wear, and my fat thighs bulged over the tops of my stockings. How I hated my thighs.

Undeterred and still playing the coquette, I lay back on the bed, kicking my legs to the music. Slowly I unbuttoned my stockings and rolled them down my legs.

I stood up again, extricated myself from the corset and was, finally, naked. My stomach felt bulbous once it was released from the tight grip of its bindings. My breasts, hanging free, were the size of enormous watermelons.

I cradled them in my folded arms and imagined

l'Inglese stroking them, kissing them, and nibbling at the nipples. I sighed.

Suddenly, emerging from my reverie, I developed goose bumps. I had the unmistakable feeling that I was being watched. Was it, could it be, Him?

Turning to the window I caught sight of Signor Rivoli, the bank manager, who lived in the opposite apartment, watching me from his balcony through the strong lenses of his spectacles.

I slammed down the blind and hurriedly slipped back into my clothes.

My body was not wonderful, but it would have to do.

CHAPTER FIVE

Monday came at last. I awoke with a stomach full of butterflies, with wings of indigo, pink, and crimson.

I got up, slipped out of my nightgown and wandered into the kitchen naked. I tied a frilly apron around myself to prevent splashes and began to prepare a pan of *maccu*, the wonderful broad bean soup, for my lunch. Something strange had happened to me. Subconsciously I was preparing myself for what was to come. Slowly but certainly my true self was throwing off its armour and was preparing to be set free. I cannot explain to you why that was so. It was something as inevitable as the birdsong and the rutting of pigs.

I slowly and carefully peeled the beans that had been soaking overnight while humming a little tune. Sometimes I smiled to myself for no particular reason. When the beans were ready I placed them in the large terracotta *pentola* with some fresh water, fennel sprigs, and sea salt. I brought them to a boil and then allowed them to simmer until tender. This takes a long time.

While the beans were simmering I got ready to go out.

In the shared bathroom I began my toilette. I stood in the little bath still singing softly and squeezed the water from my sponge on to my face and neck, my arms and breasts, stomach and legs. Thankfully, today, there was water. I dried myself well and applied cologne to my broad expanses of flesh. Snowfields of Nicolosi.

The obese Signor Placido from the floor above almost wrenched the handle off the door in his anxiety to use the bathroom.

'How much longer are you going to be in there?' he shouted.

I ignored him. When I was ready, and not before, I emerged from the bathroom clutching my robe around me, and trailing a cloud of scent that made Signor Placido sneeze as he rushed along the corridor to the bathroom.

Then I wandered back into the kitchen to stir the *maccu*, which was bubbling merrily on the little stove. Even the *maccu* was happy this morning. The very air was infected with a sense of excitement.

I dressed with care: the pink two-piece that I had made specially to honour the mayor's visit to the library in the spring of '55. Everyone had complimented me on it. Even the director. And he is not given to wasting syrupy words on the staff. Least of all me. Yes, the effect was quite pleasing. Pink certainly gives a pleasant glow to the complexion. Of course I had not forgotten the new corset; it gave my figure a lift, just as the saleslady said it would.

I stirred the pan again. It is important not to let the beans stick to the bottom and burn.

I combed my hair; the new permanent wave looked good.

I planned to leave off my little fur-lined boots. I would wear my good shoes, which were almost new. They looked so nice with the pink two-piece. I looked more like a businesswoman than a librarian. Signor Rivoli admired my appearance in the looking glass. I spied his reflection and slammed the shutters closed. Peeping Tom.

At last the beans were tender and could be squashed by the spoon against the sides of the *pentola*. I took a spoonful, blew on it gently, and tasted.

'Don't burn your tongue, Rosa. Don't spill any on the suit,' I said to myself.

A little more salt. A liberal twist of black pepper. A splash of olive oil. Delicious. This would make a most nutritious lunch served with a slice or two of a *pane rimacinato* and perhaps a little pecorino cheese. Now I was almost ready.

Just a little lipstick. There. Gorgeous. And now the dowdy mackintosh to cover it all up.

CHAPTER SIX

It was a perfect day. The pink powder-puff trees along the Via Roma were the same hue as the two-piece. They shook their heads in the breeze, casting a million petals into the air. Some fluttered in my face and lodged in my hair, giving me the appearance of a middle-aged bride.

I was trembling as I finally mounted the steps of the library. My entire life now seemed but a preparation for this day.

The doorman, Crocifisso, whistled in admiration as I came in. In the ladies' room I suddenly became afraid of appearing overdressed, and did not want to remove my raincoat. I took it off. Then put it back on. Then took it off again. This was foolish. I could not sit in my mackintosh all day. I also couldn't return home to change. I had to make the best of it and try and appear natural and normal and confident in my fine clothes.

How Costanza laughed when she saw me hiding behind the counter in the basement!

'My, Signorina Fiore, you look beautiful today. I do believe you are wearing a little lipstick. And that pink

116

suit. *So* pretty. Is it a special occasion? Are you expecting anyone in particular to come in? A man, perhaps? A foreigner? Someone who wants to look at the manuscripts?'

She tottered away shrieking with false laughter to regale the other girls with an exaggerated account of what she termed Signorina Fiore's New Look.

I locked myself in the staff lavatory and took a long look at myself in the mirror. I looked ridiculous. My fat, stupid, made-up face was staring back at me from inside the glass.

'You fool,' I said to myself, tears burning behind my eyes. 'You have made yourself look ridiculous. Look at you. Acting like a teenager. At your age. You have really given them something to laugh at now.'

I slumped down onto the seat and gave way to tears.

A knock at the door interrupted my self-recriminations.

'Oh, signorina,' came a voice I instantly recognized. 'Is that you in there? I was told it might be. Won't you come out and show me the manuscripts? It is Monday. I have my permit ready for inspection. Do come out, signorina. Please come out.'

I wiped my eyes and pinched my cheeks to give them the colour my humiliation had drained away.

'I am coming, signor; please give me a few moments.'

Then I saw the handle turning. Thankfully I had remembered to bolt the door.

'Signorina,' he whispered loudly through the crack. 'I know you're in there. Come out. Come out and get me.

'I know you want to,' he added after a pause.

I hurriedly smoothed my hair back, adjusted the pink two-piece, and unfastened the door.

When I opened it, l'Inglese stepped right up, filling the doorway so I couldn't escape. We looked into each other's eyes. I willed my eyes to hide my secrets from him, but it was too late for that now. His rich masculine scent overpowered me and made me weak. The tip of his nose touched momentarily against mine, causing a frisson that rippled out to my fingertips, my toes, the ends of my hair. His breath came deep and heavy. I knew he was breathing me, inhaling me deeply inside himself. I looked at his lips: they were moist, soft, flexing. I grew terribly hot, sweaty, and nauseous. I felt I was about to lose consciousness.

I stumbled and fell against him. He caught me and held me tightly in his arms, more tightly, perhaps, than was necessary.

'Air,' I gasped. 'I can't breathe. I need some air.'

L'Inglese hauled me from the lavatory into the wider space of the lower gallery, where he laid me down gently on the floor. Quickly he climbed on top of me and began to unfasten my blouse.

At this point the director came in. He could not believe his eyes when he saw the chaste Signorina Fiore lying spread-eagled on the floor with an unknown man seated on top and removing her clothing. His mouth fell open and his words caught in his throat. L'Inglese turned at the sound of the director's spluttering.

'No assistance is necessary, signor. I have the situation under control.'

'What are you doing to my librarian, signor?'

118

demanded the director once he had regained his composure. 'Signorina Fiore, are you all right?'

I was roused from my stupor by the sound of the director's voice.

'Oh, Signor Bandiera, I must have fainted. It is nothing. Please help me to my feet.'

Reluctantly l'Inglese relinquished his position and clambered off.

'Shall I call one of the other ladies, signorina?' asked the director, still eyeing l'Inglese with suspicion.

'No, please, signor, pray do nothing. I am quite well. I was just going to show this gentleman the manuscripts. He is a scholar. From England. He has a permit.'

'Very well, signorina, carry on, if you are sure you are well enough,' the director said with an edge to his voice as he strode across the room and stepped up the spiral staircase. I could tell my prospects of future advancement at the library had been curtailed by this episode. The director did not like surprises.

'At last, signorina, we are alone,' whispered l'Inglese into my ear.

'Now please, please,' he added imploringly, 'show me what I have long longed to feast my eyes upon. No, signorina, not that, not yet' – seeing my fingers make an unconscious movement to the remaining fastened buttons of my blouse.

'No, that later. First show me the manuscripts.'

Unsteadily I led him through the cavernous basement to the locked room where the manuscripts were contained in the aged oak cabinets specially constructed to house them. I unlocked the door with a key that hung from a chain around my girdle and switched on the special diffuse lights that do not damage the precious contents.

Carefully I removed from their cabinets the manuscripts of Archestratus, Athenaeus, and Apicius and laid them before l'Inglese, who could scarcely contain his excitement. I left him poring over them, lost in a world of ancient epicures and stupendous banquets, while I returned to my files and sharpened pencils in the outer office.

At the end of the day, l'Inglese had still not emerged from the room. As Crocifisso was locking up the various galleries, I entered the room to find l'Inglese still absorbed, making copious notes from the manuscripts in calligraphic handwriting.

'Signor, the library is now closed,' I murmured. 'It is past seven o'clock. I must ask you to finish what you are doing so I may replace the manuscripts.'

'Please, a moment longer, beautiful signorina, I have practically finished. Just a few moments more.'

I sat down and waited. Shortly l'Inglese closed the final bound copy and stretched out his arms and neck and shoulders.

'Signorina. It is done. I have completed my work on the manuscripts. A very important piece of work has been accomplished today.'

Carefully I returned the manuscripts to their cabinets, while l'Inglese gathered his things together and placed them in a little knapsack. As I was locking the cabinets, he came up very close behind me and buried his face in the back of my neck, making small, whimpering animal noises.

'Ahh, signorina. It has been a long hard day's work for the poor Inglese. Won't you comfort him just a little?'

'Signor, it is past closing time. If we do not hurry we will be locked in overnight.'

'That would not be so bad, signorina, would it?' he whispered right inside my ear.

'Signor, please, I must go,' I said, freeing myself.

'Very well, Miss Independent.'

L'Inglese stood back gallantly and with a wonderful gesture of his aristocratic hand waved me ahead of him up the spiral staircase. I had reached halfway before I realized that he had positioned himself directly underneath and was looking up my skirts. I tried to gather the material close around my legs so he could not see anything, but in truth, he had already seen everything. He smiled broadly at my discomfort.

As we walked through the entrance hall I knew I had to speak soon or I would always regret it. I had to be brave and speak out. I could not let this moment go by; I had to seize it. I knew I had reached a turning point in my life, and the next few seconds would be critical.

'Of course, signor,' I said very quickly, as if afraid my courage would desert me at the last moment, 'if you really want to know about our food, you will not find it in books.'

'No?' L'Inglese read the signal.

'You, um, you need someone to show you.' I looked at him squarely while blushing like a beetroot.

'You mean you cook, signorina?' he asked, his eyes bright with a sudden fire.

'Signor,' I said, 'I cook.'

'Of course,' he replied, tapping his forehead with his little hand in a gesture of sudden and complete realization. 'Of course, now everything falls into place. It is natural, it is right that you cook, signorina. How could I not realize this from the beginning? From the moment when first I placed my eyes upon you and drew you into my soul like a breath.'

As he was saying this l'Inglese placed his little hands in an elaborate gesture upon his midriff, where his soul apparently lay.

'Teach me, signorina,' he breathed. 'Teach me everything. I will be your pupil, your disciple, your slave.'

He removed one of his hands from his midriff and placed it on my generous breast. I groaned.

'Teach me. Oh, teach me, signorina, say that you will.'

I was incapable of uttering a word. My vocal cords, along with my other organs, seemed to be in a state of paralysis. Already I was experiencing doubts. I felt myself a novice swimmer in very deep water. Still, I had spoken out; now there was no turning back.

'Ttchurggh,' I gurgled, by way of response.

'Tchurrgg . . . ?' repeated l'Inglese. This was a word that was new to him.

'I'm sorry, signorina, what is it, the ttchuuurggh?'

'Forgive me, signor,' finding my voice at last, 'I have a little hoarseness in my throat. I will do what I can to assist you.'

'Signorina, you make me the happiest of men,' he said

while bowing and, at the same time, hiding a little smile.

As I hurried home through the darkening streets, my heart fluttering, I had the feeling that I was being followed. I kept looking over my shoulder after every few paces but did not catch sight of anyone. I suppose I was just feeling unsettled. Had I been too forward in speaking out? I had almost shocked myself: it was as though someone else, someone bold and unafraid, had been acting for me.

I spent another sleepless night in my apartment and in the early hours of the morning I stole once more into my little kitchen, to prepare a huge *torta di ricotta*. I needed a cheesecake: it was the only thing that could give me the peace of mind I craved.

Had I been too hasty in offering to give l'Inglese lessons? I asked myself, as I ground green almonds with my pestle. The power of my wrist quickly turned the almonds to powder. If only I could grind my worries away as easily.

I beat the ricotta, egg yolks, honey, sugar, lemon juice, and rind into the almonds. I beat and beat and beat the mixture until a sweat formed on my brow and my body began to glow with warmth. Even then I did not stop beating. I welcomed the exhaustion that began to creep up on me: I could feel the healing power of my cooking.

Really I knew nothing about l'Inglese. Nothing at all. Except that everything about him spelled danger to an inexperienced woman like me. I was afraid of him, yet could not bear the thought of not seeing him again. I was always thinking of him, imagining our next meeting: amusing myself with every possible scenario.

I whisked the egg whites into peaks in a matter of seconds. I reasoned that I had been right to speak out to him when I did. I knew how I would have hated myself if I had let the moment slip by. I knew how wretched and foolish I would have felt at my impotence, and yet this turbulence inside me was almost as bad. Acrobatic butterflies fluttered in my stomach, however much I tried to feed them into submission.

When the *torta* had baked to a golden, angel-scented crust, and after waiting impatiently for it to cool, I helped myself to a large slice with a thick dollop of cream. Ooh, it was good. I mopped up every crumb from the plate with my finger. Then I switched out the lights and climbed back into bed. I resigned myself to the thought that what was done could not be undone and drifted into a lemon-flavoured sleep.

The following day I took the remains of the *torta* into the library to feed the poor students who did not bring any lunch. I always did this when I made anything I could not eat all alone. I reserved a large portion for Crocifisso, the doorman, to take home for his family. I could only guess how he fed his wife and seven *bambini* on the money he made.

L'Estate

THE SUMMER

CHAPTER ONE

We had arranged to meet at the corner of the Via Cala and the Via Cassari in the middle of the Vucciria market. When I arrived, l'Inglese was already there, trying to avoid dirtying his dainty shoes by stepping in the running water, discarded entrails, glistening fish parts, and the other foul detritus of market life.

I had been to the Per Donna hair parlour. My hair had been back-combed, sprayed, and piled so high it resembled a creation of the seventeenth-century French court. Unfortunately, when I emerged from the salon it was drizzling slightly and the pile of hair had sunk like a failed soufflé before setting like cement.

We were instinctively aware of each other's presence. Around us whirled the din of the market: the cries of the fish filleters, the vegetable sellers, and the butchers, the gabble of the housewives and the clucking of short-lived chickens. The accordion player vied with the rumbling of carts and the braying of mules. Yet a bubble of silence surrounded l'Inglese and me.

He kissed my hand without speaking and then we

drifted through the tumult in slow motion like characters in a silent film.

An amazing thing was taking place in the air between our bodies, something that flowed from both and entered each, joining us in a sticky web. It swelled and expanded, plucking at the strings of the deep-seated place in each of us that yearned and ached for consummation of this thing that had overcome us. Overhead the red awnings of the merchants bulged and flapped like the wings of a great red bird. Inside me a red wound throbbed.

We wandered the entire length of the street market, stopping to buy the provisions I needed for the lunch dish I wanted to prepare to initiate l'Inglese into the real art of Sicilian cuisine.

I took l'Inglese around the best stalls, teaching him how to choose produce, livestock, game, fish, and meat of the highest quality for his dishes.

Together we circled among the vegetable sellers, who were praising their heaps of artichokes, courgettes still bearing their yellow flowers, spikes of asparagus, purple-tinged cauliflowers, oyster mushrooms, and vine tomatoes with their customary cries:

'Carciofi fresci.'

'Funghi belli.'

'Tutto economico.'

I squeezed and pinched, sniffed, and weighed things in my hands, and having agreed on the goods I would then haggle over the price. The stallholders were used to me, but they had never known me to be accompanied by a man.

Wild strawberries, cherries, oranges and lemons, quinces and melons were all subject to my scrutiny.

The olive sellers, standing behind their huge basins containing all varieties of olives in brine, oil, or vinegar, called out to me:

'Hey, Rosa, who's your friend?'

We made our way to the meat vendors, where rabbits fresh from the fields, huge sides of beef, whole pigs and sheep were hung up on hooks, and offal and tripe were spread out on marble slabs. I selected some chicken livers, which were wrapped in paper and handed to l'Inglese to carry. I had never had a man to carry my shopping before; it made me feel special.

We passed the stalls where whole tuna fish, sardines and oysters, whitebait and octopuses were spread out, reflecting the abundant sea surrounding our island. Fish was not on the menu today, but nevertheless I wanted to show l'Inglese where to find the finest tuna, the freshest shrimps, and the most succulent swordfish in the whole market.

After we completed our shopping we walked back together down the Corso Vittorio Emanuel. Occasionally he would brush his hand or arm against me and I would experience a jolt of electricity.

CHAPTER TWO

It was not without embarrassment that I admitted l'Inglese into my little apartment in the Via Vicolo Brugno. Naturally, the day before I had sought permission from Nonna Frolla to give cooking lessons to a foreign gentleman in my apartment.

'I see no reason why the gentleman should not call, Rosa, *for cooking classes*,' Nonna had said with emphasis.

'Of course I shall call in to introduce myself, as your landlady. I assume he will be leaving before evening?'

'Of course, Nonna,' I said, blushing like a teenager.

Nonna had hurried to her husband with this news. It proved what she had known all along. That there was a man in my life, and a foreigner, too. She would keep her one good eye open the next day; of that Signor Frolla could be sure.

I opened the door and admitted l'Inglese inside.

'Here, signor, is *la cucina*,' I showed him. 'Of course, it is very different from a proper country kitchen, such as the one on my family's farm. Still, I have everything here that I need.'

'I can see that, signorina,' he said.

L'Inglese immediately made himself at home, examining my copper pots and testing the sharpness of my knives while undressing me with his eyes.

'And where, signorina, is the bedroom?' he asked after a pause.

I pretended not to have heard the question, and assuming a businesslike posture I rolled up my sleeves and put on my apron.

I wanted to show him how to make a *timballo*. This baroque dish exemplifies the style of cooking from the island's aristocratic past, known as *cucina baronale*. Its main ingredient is macaroni, which, until the eighteenth century, was a celebratory food that only the very wealthy could afford to eat. The macaroni is mixed with mushrooms, onions, tomato paste, chicken livers, wine, cheese, and ham and then formed into a pie with a melting pastry crust. It is a complicated dish, so we tend to make it only on special occasions.

First I prepared the pastry dough. I stood back to let l'Inglese knead it and as he moved closer I could feel his breath on my cheek. I inhaled his cologne. Our fingertips met in the mixing bowl. Momentarily I stopped breathing; it was one of the most erotic moments of my life.

L'Inglese's lips puckered slightly and he reached forward slowly. There was a knock on the door.

'It's my landlady,' I said apologetically.

'Let's keep very quiet and she won't know we're in here,' he suggested conspiratorially as he tried to draw me down under the table to hide.

'Oh, she knows we're here, signor; she has only one

good eye, but it sees like a hawk. I will have to let her in or there will be trouble.'

I dusted off my hands with a cloth and opened the door. Nonna Frolla trotted in along with her pug.

'Sir, I am Donna Maria Frolla, grocer and landlady. I understand that you are taking cooking lessons from my tenant Signorina Fiore.'

'That is true, most excellent lady,' said l'Inglese, immediately exerting his charm by kissing her clawlike hand. Nonna Frolla was enchanted and immediately began to play the part of a 111-year-old coquette.

'Signor, please,' Nonna said with exaggerated formality, drawing her hand away.

'I, unlike my tenant, am a married woman. Signor, it is my duty to protect my dwelling from the merest hint, the merest smirch of dishonour. I am sure you will understand that in my business my reputation is all-important.'

She sat herself down and continued, 'Sir, I have been like a mother to Signorina Fiore for the past twenty-five years, since she first came into my lodgings, and I take responsibility to protect her and guide her through the villainous, the tortuous alleyways of life. She is very naive, signor. She is not one of us Palermitians; she is from the country, out in the east where their ways are very primitive, very different from ours. May I ask you, signor, what your intentions are towards my tenant?'

'Signora, I thank you for your concern for the welfare of your charming tenant and daughter Signorina Fiore. May I assure you that my intentions are more than honourable. I intend to take lessons from her. That is all.'

'Of course, signor, of course, you are right. You are an

honourable man. That is plain to see to anyone who looks into your honest face. Forgive me for being so careful. But I am sure you appreciate the sincerity of my motives in securing the reputation of this poor lonely girl. There are men, signor, of a type unknown to you I am sure, who would take advantage of such a girl; a girl of such naiveté and large bosoms. Bear me no ill will, signor, if I seek to protect her. Now, I see that you want to get on with your lessons. Please don't let me interrupt you any longer. It has been a pleasure meeting you, signor. I hope we may welcome you here again.'

'Signora,' said l'Inglese, suppressing a smile, 'may I assure you the pleasure has been all mine.'

Simpering, the signora bowed her way out backwards and ran back to the shop to give all her customers a verbal portrait of l'Inglese.

I was furious with Nonna Frolla for talking about me to l'Inglese this way. I would speak to her about it later. The embarrassment of it.

L'Inglese laughed at my pained expression.

'Signorina, you did not tell me that you lived in a convent.'

We returned to our work. Once the dough was mixed we set it aside to rest while we prepared the filling of pasta, mushrooms, and silky chicken livers.

'Taking some dried porcini mushrooms,' I said, imitating the cookery shows I had heard on the radio, 'you should soak them in enough warm water to cover them fully and leave them for half an hour. Gradually they will soften and expand, releasing an acrid aroma and colouring the water a rich brown.'

Now was the time to make macaroni. I took little pieces of the dough we had prepared together and showed l'Inglese how to roll them around special straws called *busi* so that they form a tube. Then the fingers carefully release them.

This took much longer than I had anticipated, as l'Inglese deliberately ruined his macaroni again and again. I had to take his hands in mine to demonstrate the rolling motion an infinite number of times.

'While the mushrooms are soaking and the dough is relaxing,' I continued, 'sauté a small chopped onion in a little olive oil until it is soft and transparent. Add some *'strattu*, or strong tomato paste, and cook for a few minutes. Add two handfuls of chicken livers and cook until they just begin to colour. Add a little white wine and the mushrooms with the water they've soaked in, and cook for about twenty minutes. Signor, please, don't do that,' removing his hands from my bottom as I faced the stove.

'What shall we do while it is cooking, signorina? Perhaps you could show me the rest of your charming apartment?'

'This is all there is, signor.'

'Surely, signorina, you do not sleep in this kitchen?'

'I have a small bedroom, obviously, signor.'

'Ah, a bedroom. Won't you show me?'

'No, signor. Now we need to add a good measure of butter to the pan and season the mixture with salt and pepper. Next, we need to cook the macaroni in plenty of salted boiling water until it is al dente. To test for this, you should literally bite a piece of the pasta and feel its texture against your teeth, thus . . .' I demonstrated.

'Signorina, do you know that you have the most sensuous mouth that I have ever seen?'

'If the macaroni is ready, drain and mix with some more butter, some grated *parmigiano*, and some prosciutto cut into thick strips; then mix all of this into the liver and mushroom mixture, so.'

He was still scrutinizing my mouth, with his own slightly opened and reaching forward. He was in danger of catching flies in it, and I told him so.

'Finally, oil a *timballo* mould and line the base and sides with two-thirds of the pastry dough. Fill it with the macaroni mixture, then cover with the rest of the pastry and brush with some beaten egg. Cook in a moderate oven for around half an hour until the pastry is golden.'

With the *timballo* safely in the stove, l'Inglese pounced. He was not going to be put off any longer. He seized me in his arms and delivered a passionate kiss on the sensuous mouth of this startled librarian. I fought for breath.

The most wonderful aroma was filling the air, causing those passing through the street outside to look up and say: 'Rosa is in her kitchen today, there's no mistaking it.'

'What's the matter? Signorina, why, you kiss like a frightened mouse. Just relax, open your lips, let your tongue stray into my mouth, it is nice, come, let me show you.'

He seized me again, but I was too nervous, and too embarrassed at my ineptitude and lack of experience. Accidentally I bit him, causing him to yowl.

'Signorina, signorina, kiss with the lips, with the tongue, not with the teeth.'

'Let us make a salad, signor, I think the *timballo* is almost ready.'

'Signorina, don't be frightened. Let yourself go. I know you want to.'

And so I kissed him. Tentatively at first, but as my confidence grew I softened my lips and gently proffered my tongue, which he received in his mouth, licking it with his own. It was a beautiful moment.

The smell of smoke interrupted the kiss. The *timballo* was burning. I snatched it from the oven. Fortunately only the crust was blackened.

'Signor, this won't do,' I said crossly. '*La cucina* is a serious business, we must give it all our attention, for if we don't you see what happens. The dish knows she is being ignored, and she punishes us.'

'Signorina, soon you will see that the arts of *amore e cucina* complement one another perfectly. Indeed they are part of the same thing: the celebration of life. We should not sacrifice one to the other.'

I released the angry *timballo* from its mould, and we waited impatiently for it to cool a little. Finally we sat down to lunch at the kitchen table. We also had green salad, some Regaliali wine, and some fine bread, which I had to admit I didn't make, but bought from the Crosta Brothers Panetteria in the Via Volturno, near the Teatro Massimo. It was almost as good as my own bread, but not quite.

L'Inglese lifted a forkful of the *timballo* to his lips. He tasted and then closed his eyes.

'What is the matter, signor,' I asked anxiously, 'is it not good?'

'Signorina,' he said, licking his lips luxuriantly, 'it is sublime.'

L'Inglese then abandoned his fork and began to eat with his fingers.

'To eat like this, signorina, gives me so much more pleasure,' he said, licking some crumbs of pastry from his fingers.

'Like this,' he continued, 'I can feel the texture of the food with my fingertips. I become much more intimately involved with the dish. The hard metal fork is not for me. No. I like to touch the food, to smell it' – here he inhaled deeply – 'I like to feel it against my skin, not just in my mouth. Food is such a sensuous thing, eating is such a sensuous pleasure. Eating good food, signorina, is akin to lovemaking. It should be enjoyed, not rushed. We should abandon ourselves to its sensuality, signorina. Now I take again a piece of the wonderful *timballo*. I feel its warmth between my fingers; I feel the soft succulence of the filling, the glorious crust of the pastry. I place it on my tongue slowly, lovingly. I draw it inside my mouth and experience the frisson as my taste buds go to work. I lick my fingers to enjoy every last little bit of it. My fingers brush against my tongue, my lips, flesh against flesh. Now, signorina, I want you to try it.'

I put down my fork and pulled a piece from the *timballo* with my fingers. I raised it to my lips.

'Slowly, slowly, don't rush it.'

I opened my mouth.

'Yes, yes.'

And placed it inside.

'Now, signorina, let your mouth close over it slowly,

that's right. Feel it with the soft part of your mouth, with your tongue. Slowly, slowly begin to chew. Feel the texture of the food inside your mouth. Don't rush it, enjoy it. When you are ready, swallow. Lick your lips, that's right, now your fingers. Let your fingers linger on your lips for a moment. Slowly draw your forefinger across the inside of your lower lip. Doesn't that feel nice? Now, signorina, I want you to feed me.'

'Oh no, signor, I couldn't.'

'Why ever not?'

'It wouldn't be proper.'

'Nonsense, signorina. Now do it.'

And so I did it. I broke off a piece of the pastry crust with my fingers and with it scooped a tasty morsel of filling. It felt warm and moist and silky. With a slightly trembling hand I reached across the little table to where l'Inglese was waiting. He parted his lips. They were red and wet. He opened his mouth wider. I saw his bad teeth and his pink tongue. I reached further towards him. He reached towards me with his mouth open. I proffered the morsel of *timballo*. I put it on his tongue and he drew it inside his mouth. As I withdrew my hand he caught it roughly at the wrist. He began to chew slowly, with his eyes closed, still holding my wrist firmly. After swallowing, he drew my hand towards him and sucked at my fingers, licking along their entire length before drawing the tips into his mouth. It was just as in my dream.

'Now, signorina, I will feed you.'

And he did.

I blushed as he lifted the food to my mouth and

touched my lips with his fingers; once I had chewed slowly and swallowed, he inserted his fingers into my mouth.

'Suck them, signorina,' he ordered.

I had to obey. He closed his eyes with the pleasure of a stroked cat.

I had grease and a little trickle of saliva on my chin. He reached across the table and licked me clean.

We continued with our meal, feeding one another slowly across the little table. The room seemed to grow warmer. When the food was finished and the bottle of wine was empty, I tried rousing myself to reality. I cleared the table and began to wash the dishes. As I stood at the little sink, l'Inglese came up behind me and pressed himself against me. I could feel something hard through his trousers. It almost hurt as he pressed it against me.

'Signorina, I must have you,' he whispered in my hair just above my ear. 'We must make love now, this instant. I must have you. I cannot take another refusal.'

'Signor, really, I cannot,' I stammered, breathing heavily.

'What do you mean you cannot?' he erupted, finally losing his temper and speaking with a genuine anger. 'You get me so excited, so aroused that I feel as though I will explode, and then you deny me the natural release for my feelings. You reject me. What do you think you are doing? Don't pretend you don't know. You are fully aware of what you are doing to me. You tease me, tease me beyond the point of no return. What am I to be played with? We are not adolescents. If you deny me now I will go straight out of here and find a whore on whom to vent my frustrations, and you, signorina, will never see me again.'

'Please, not so loud, signor, I implore you. They are listening . . .'

'I don't give a fuck who is listening.'

'Signor, signor, please. Not here. I cannot do it here. We are surrounded, we are watched. Look . . .'

I pointed from the window. Sure enough Signor Rivoli the bank manager was glued to his window on the opposite side of the street, his trousers were around his ankles, and he was masturbating with a stupid grin on his face.

'What, a Peeping Tom?' cried l'Inglese; he seemed about to break the window with his fist. Signor Rivoli scuttled away from the window, showing his bare bottom as he tried not to trip over his trousers before he disappeared from view.

'What kind of a place is this? It is full of mad people. How can you live in such a place? So, you will not do it here, you say. Very well, signorina, where will you do it?'

'I don't know, signor. I just cannot do it here. I feel so hampered here.'

'Very well, signorina, we will go to my villa; but if we get there and you again refuse me I will go quite mad.'

He seized me by the arm and pulled me out of my apartment. I did not even have time to pick up my bag or a sweater. As he ripped open the door he almost demolished the tiny form of Nonna Frolla, who crouched there, and who had obviously been peering through the keyhole.

'Seen anything interesting, signora?' he asked as we rushed past.

'Well, really, the rudeness of it . . .' she said to the pug in the now empty hallway.

CHAPTER THREE

L'Inglese was taking me to a villa in the Via Belmonte, in the district of Acquasanta, far out to the north of the city, on a cliff overlooking the harbour.

After we left my apartment we jumped into a chaise waiting outside the duomo. I knew that I had gone beyond the point of no return. I knew that now I had to give myself to him. And the curious thing is that I realized for the first time that I wanted to.

As we drove away from the city I allowed myself to feel the excitement of that definitive moment without guilt. I was now throwing off the shackles I had borne for so long, which had only started loosening since my first encounter with l'Inglese. Was that really only last week? Was it not time to discard the straitjacket of conventional morality? What had I done with my life for the last twenty-five years? Why should I not live a little, and if not now, then when? What did I have to lose?

Here was a man who wanted me, and in the course of my entire life there had only been one other: Bartolomeo.

But I was little more than a child then, that summer a lifetime ago.

When the time came, I decided, not only would I give myself to him without reservation, but I would reach out and take him for myself too. What a change had come over the librarian!

We arrived at the villa. L'Inglese's hand holding mine was hot and sweaty. Could it be that he was nervous too?

As the drive swept around from the road, the house emerged in the distance, set against the sparkling sea. It was beautiful: very white in the sun, surrounded by a magical garden of palms and lemons and lilies.

'It's beautiful. Is it yours?'

'No, it belongs to a friend of mine. He lets me stay here. He never uses it himself.'

The chaise left us at the steps and drove away. As it receded into the distance I felt suddenly vulnerable, realizing that no-one knew my whereabouts. But of course the cabdriver knew. He was one of Nonna Frolla's customers and would make his report in the morning when he bought his prosciutto.

Together we mounted the steps, and suddenly became quite shy. Inside, the entrance hall, cavernous and sparkling with white marble, looked like a *cassata*.

Not even taking time to look around, I fell on l'Inglese, taking him by surprise. Scared that my courage would fail me, I kissed him hard on the lips. Miraculously, the frightened mouse disappeared.

He had not expected this, and he thought he knew women. He kissed me back and we sucked and sucked at one another, paddling with our hungry tongues. Madly, deeply, desperately we kissed in the hall of the marble palace, and the pent-up force of the twelve days of longing overcame us.

As we kissed, our hands roved over the expanse of our bodies, now our world. We pulled wildly but ineffectually at clothes, belts, buckles, buttons, and fastenings. Frustrated, I ripped l'Inglese's shirt from his waistband.

Not to be outdone, he ripped my dress, leaving the sleeves in place, but the central panel came away in his hands.

Struggling not to lose the fusion of the kiss amid this activity, we tore at what remained of each other's clothing. We hurried to remove it, as a lifesaver would before diving into the river to rescue a drowning child.

With one final heave, which left me weakened, I managed to release l'Inglese's belt buckle, which was clamped under his balcony stomach. His blue jeans were stiff and the metal buttons so difficult to undo. My deft fingers that made pasta shapes were strong and supple, they wheedled and wrenched until the buttons released and the fly succumbed to expose a throbbing bulge clad in black silk undershorts.

Still we maintained the vacuum between our two mouths. Indeed, as the intensity grew, our urgency was increased.

I tore at the blue jeans, peeling them away from his bottom, and using one of my feet I pushed them down l'Inglese's legs. They remained trapped around his ankles. He was still wearing his shoes. At my next lunge he toppled over and together we crashed onto the marble floor, hurting but laughing. It was the first time we had laughed together, and this broke the tension of what could otherwise have been a ridiculous moment.

Then we again fell to tearing and plucking. We were desperate to get out of the clothes that were enveloping us, sticking to us so persistently like used chewing gum discarded on the pavement.

L'Inglese tore off my shoes and tossed them aside. They slid over the smooth marble tiles with a skidding sound before finally coming to rest. His were more tricky; they had laces and the laces were tied in double bows. Those were the shoes that first seduced me: I had always been attracted to brogues.

Finally I managed to wrench them off; in doing so I broke a nail; it ricocheted across the room. He flailed his legs madly to remove the blue jeans, which had become his bitter enemy. Get off, get off.

Then l'Inglese disposed of the tattered remains of my dress; the orphaned sleeves were torn from my arms, and the rags tossed away; they lassoed the form of a marble Venus who was watching, shocked, from a niche in the wall.

Silk slip, ripped.

Stockings followed.

Then he discovered that I was vacuum-packed in a corset of such resilience that it twanged like a trampoline and repelled any advance. Its material was so durable that it couldn't be ripped, and its force of suction was so great that it couldn't be removed. It was the colour of salmon paste and he thought it was the most revolting thing he had ever seen.

145

'Christ, what is this thing? Did your landlady make you wear it? Wait here, I know how to get it off.'

L'Inglese got up from the floor and rushed off, sliding like an ice-skater on the marble in his socks. Socks always spoil a love scene. There never is a right time to take them off.

Seconds later he reappeared brandishing a vegetable knife. It was of the highest quality, fine tempered steel, foreign, of course. I had always coveted such a knife. That was my first thought. My second was what he intended to do with it. My fear must have shown in my face.

'Be still, signorina, be calm. Lie down, I will not harm you. I must remove this abominable corset, that is all.'

'But signor . . .'

'No buts, signorina, trust me. I am an excellent filleter.'

He knelt alongside me as I stretched out on the marble floor.

'Keep very, very still.'

I closed my eyes.

Slowly he inserted the blade under the join between the enormous cups at my cleavage.

I was hardly able to breathe.

He made the first incision, concentrating like a surgeon. There was a fizzing sound as the pressure was released and the rubberized cloth split open. Following a straight line along the length of my body he slit the garment from my breasts, down to my stomach, and finally to my crotch.

The corset popped open, delivering my naked form

like a monstrous pea from its pod. I looked for blood.
There wasn't any.

When the tension was over, we could both laugh.
Not many people have heard my laugh; it is fruity and
deep and bubbles up from somewhere far inside me.
L'Inglese's laugh was like that of a horse; it was so funny
it made me laugh even more.

I realized I was naked as l'Inglese feasted his eyes on
my body. I could almost feel my skin scorching under his
glance.

'God, you're beautiful,' he said.

And he meant it; and I was; and I felt it, then, for the
first time in my life. I basked in it: in his praise and my
beauty.

I lay back, watching him watching me as he removed
his socks and his tattered shirt. I already loved the
movements of his hands, the way he lit and smoked a
cigarette or tied his shoelaces; so elegant, so polished. I
was impatient to experience all that those hands would
do to me.

His body, almost bare, was soft and white and warm
and furry, a contrast to the cool, smooth silk of his
underpants, which were all that remained in place. Then
they came off too. I stared blatantly. I could tell l'Inglese
was flattered.

'Now, signorina, let us go to my room; we will be more
comfortable there than on this hard stone floor.'

L'Inglese took my hand and, naked as the nymphs
cavorting on the frieze above our heads, we ran up the
sweeping staircase to the *primo piano* and the bedrooms.

CHAPTER FOUR

My clothes had been ripped to shreds the previous evening. I had to borrow a pair of l'Inglese's linen trousers
and a shirt in which to return home. My corset had been
sliced through with the vegetable knife, so I did not even
have any *intimo*.

I could barely walk from the vigour of the activities
of the night before. I was exhausted and euphoric. As
I limped along I smiled broadly, sometimes laughing,
sometimes blushing at the recollection of our lovemaking.
Sometimes I groaned out loud as I relived each orgasm.

Yet as I approached my little street my mood began to
change. I knew how Nonna Frolla and her neighbours
would greet me. By now, they would know everything. I
already felt the weight of their condemnation.

And so I returned, feeling like a slut, to the Via Vicolo
Brugno. I could feel pairs of eyes watching me as I
turned, limping slightly, into the street. There was no
getting away from the gossip, from having your personal
life exposed. I thought Palermo would be different
from Castiglione in that respect, but I was wrong. Here,

people had even more time for gossip, and once again I had made myself its target.

'Disgraceful behaviour,' said Signor Manzini, a retired schoolteacher and the bridge partner of Nonno Frolla for the past seventy-eight years. 'I always thought Signorina Fiore was a decent young woman, but like all the rest she turns out to be a whore.'

'Disgraceful is right,' agreed Signor Rivoli, the bank manager, popping into the shop for his *caciocavallo* cheese and olives. 'You should have seen the things they were doing in there. I was shocked, I tell you, totally shocked. She could not control herself; she's a slut, no doubt about that . . .'

'So you were watching, were you?'

'Well, er . . .'

'Peeping Tom.'

'Pervert.'

'Disgraceful.'

'Disgusting.'

Signor Rivoli was hounded out of the shop.

There was an air of expectation in the street: not only had I behaved like a whore, staying away from home in the company of a stranger *and* a foreigner, but in addition, during my absence, a letter had arrived, express delivery, addressed to me. The fact that this letter arrived on an extraordinary day was interpreted as a portent of bad news.

Express delivery was most unusual. Why would normal delivery not do? As the letter lay on the counter all morning awaiting my arrival, all customers were called upon to speculate and comment on it.

Quinto Cavallo, the goldsmith, had taken the liberty of examining the postmark, but it was smudged and gave no clue. The handwriting was equally anonymous. Quinto was able to cite the example of his brother's friend's neighbour's acquaintance in Agrigento who had received a similar letter that bore very bad news, the worst news possible, but no-one believed him.

The hairdresser, Bernardino Capelli, from the Corso Ruggero, was intent on steaming it open, but this Nonna Frolla would not permit; she drew the line at actually opening her tenants' letters.

All lay in wait for me. When I finally appeared around the corner of the Via Bologna, Fredo the butcher's boy ran in to alert those in the shop.

'Nonna Frolla, she's coming, the whore's coming down the street.'

'That's enough, boy,' Nonna rebuked him with a slap to the cheek. 'You keep quiet.'

Nonna smoothed her hair and skirts in anticipation of trouble. The customers in the shop suddenly became animated and started to talk like characters on a stage when the curtains open. To their collective disappointment I walked straight past the shop, nose in the air, without even looking in.

Nonna Frolla whisked up the letter from the counter and gave chase. She was surprisingly nimble for a woman of 111.

'Rosa, Rosa,' she called, puffing gently. The pug puffed louder, trying to keep up.

I looked around.

'Rosa, what has happened to you? Where are your clothes? You look as though you have been the victim of an attack. Where have you been, dear? I've been so worried about you.'

'I'm fine, Nonna, there really is no need for you to worry about me.'

'Been with that gentleman, I suppose?'

I chose to ignore the question.

'I am in a hurry, Nonna, do you want anything in particular?'

'As a matter of fact I do,' snapped Nonna Frolla, her tone of fake concern evaporating. 'I haven't the time to chase around after my tenants when there's nothing particular. Staying out all night in the company of strange men, bringing a bad name to my house, upsetting my tenants, wouldn't have been countenanced in my day. It is absolutely disgraceful. Of all of this I say nothing. But while you were out doing whatever it is you have been doing, all night, with him, that man, that foreigner, an important letter has been delivered for you. I discharge my duties as landlady, I put myself last, I sacrifice myself to the will of my tenants. The reputation of my house is destroyed by the actions of this brazen girl, but still I deliver her mail . . .'

I took the letter from Nonna's hand and, simply saying 'Thank you,' I disappeared inside my apartment and shut the door.

I immediately recognized my mother's handwriting. My mother had written me in Palermo only once before, and that was twenty years ago now. That first letter had informed me that she had shot Antonino Calabrese after discovering him in the cowshed with the dairymaid Balbina Burgondofara.

Certainly Mama was not one for needless letter writing; this letter also had to mean bad news. In haste I tore it open. It read as follows:

'Rosa, *figlia mia*,

I have had a telegram from your brother Luigi in Chicago. He has heard from his associates that you are behaving like a whore, and have got mixed up in the company of some *Inglese*. You must stop it immediately, for he says he cannot have a stain on the family honour. I say to you Rosa you must stop your whorish behaviour or I don't know what will happen.

With my best wishes

Your mother

Isabella Calabrese'

Immediately there was a tap on the front door. I opened it to discover Nonna Frolla outside.

'Was it bad news?' she asked with hope in her voice.

I simply shut the door again. Outside Nonna could be heard muttering, but I ignored her.

How could the news travel so fast to Luigi in Chicago? I knew he had been successful in the States, had become a businessman with his own chain of pizza restaurants. I knew he had connections; but how could his 'associates' know about me?

What Mama said sounded almost like a threat. I did not take it seriously, of course, but it was puzzling. This business of family honour too. Even when he was still in Castiglione, Luigi was not concerned with that. It was all very strange.

My thoughts began to chase their tails until they became blurred. I recognized the signs and saw it was time to take out my pans. Preparing a dish always helped me to think more clearly. Besides, I was ravenously hungry. The delicious *pasticcio di Sostanza* was sufficiently complicated to give me enough time to consider the facts.

First I kneaded a rich pastry dough and set it aside to relax. Then I took a plump corn-fed chicken that I had hanging in my larder, and setting it down upon my butcher's block I took a cleaver to it, splitting the bones with a fizz as the blade whistled through the air and came down with a thud. How good it felt to chop away like this: one of the things I missed most about the *fattoria* was butchering the animals I had slaughtered. When we were children growing up, my brothers wanted to be cowboys or postmen: I, however, wanted to be a butcher.

I kept returning to thoughts of l'Inglese. How did Luigi know about him? I browned the chicken pieces in some good olive oil, and when they were done I fried the onion in the same oil, to ensure I had captured all the flavour of the fowl.

Then I added parsley, some tomatoes, finely chopped, salt, pepper, and a good-sized bay leaf. I returned the chicken pieces to the pot and left it to simmer.

Luigi had spies in Palermo, that was obvious: but I was not presumptuous enough to think he would have them keep a watch over me. I was of no interest to the Mafia.

I sliced thinly through the chicken's innards with a sharp cook's knife. How I loved the delicate feel of livers between my fingers. I sautéed these in butter with the heart and gizzards and they released a bewitching aroma, which, out in the street, caused the passers-by to close their eyes and inflate their nostrils.

'She may be a whore,' I heard Signor Manzini saying beneath my window, 'but she knows how to cook.'

Perhaps I was looking at things the wrong way. Perhaps it was l'Inglese they were interested in. I cannot explain why that thought came to me and took hold as I crumbled some fresh sausage into the smoking oil and watched it bubble. I added a little red wine and some fresh tomato sauce, some salt and a grind of pepper. I almost added too much pepper, for while my mind rotated on this premise, my wrist continued to twist the head of the pepper mill. But my skill was such that I subconsciously stopped just in time.

I lined the pie dish with the pastry. Despite my obsession with l'Inglese, I had to admit I knew almost nothing about him. I placed a layer of the chicken meat in the pastry case and sprinkled over a little cinnamon and a little sugar.

I had no reason to suppose he was involved with the Mafia. But the idea kept grating away at me. It just seemed to fit.

Next, a layer of sausage. More cinnamon. Mmmmmm. Wonderful fragrant powder. He had told me he was a scholar, but what did that really mean? Giblets. Then chicken again. Then sausage. Then giblets. Suddenly I felt scared.

I poured tomato sauce over the top and stretched the pastry lid over the dish. Then I sealed the edges with a finger dipped in water and a few deft pinches.

Now that I had found love again, this late in my life,

why was fate so cruel to me? Could this man too be connected with *la famiglia*? Despite having been born with teeth in my mouth, I was cursed with ill luck.

Before popping the *pasticcio* in a hot oven, I made a slash at the top with a knife to release the steam and brushed it with a beaten egg yolk.

I sat down at the table and looked out of the window. He was out there, somewhere, not far away. My soul somehow reached out to him. I knew the dangers. I was certainly not going to take Mama's advice and end the relationship, but I would need to be on my guard.

CHAPTER FIVE

Our lessons continued throughout that glorious summer, though at the villa rather than at my apartment; Nonna Frolla's interference and the gossip of the neighbours gave me no peace, and I was afraid that l'Inglese's violent temper might provoke him to do something awful if he ever came there again.

The weather was perfect, hot white days and warm sultry nights: weather for cooks and lovers. The produce in the market was now at its finest: everything ripened by the intensity of the sun, the flavours richer, the odours more pungent, and the colours brighter than at any other time.

It was, I decided, the right time to make the *'strattu*, a traditional tomato paste, made outdoors and found only in Sicily. Nowadays the trouble of making it deters all but the most dedicated of cooks. I had not made *'strattu* since I was a girl back at *la fattoria*, and I thought it would be a good learning exercise for l'Inglese, who, it seemed to me, was far too impatient to be a true Sicilian cook.

He complained loudly as I insisted that he carry a whole sack of ripe tomatoes back from the Vucciria market. They were an almost fluorescent red in colour from the heat of the sun, bursting with juices and their wonderful perfume: warmth, sunlight, fertile earth, summer, rain. L'Inglese was a similar colour as he struggled with them up the hill to the villa, cursing loudly.

He made more fuss when I made him chop them all and pass them through the fine mesh of a sieve to remove the peel and the seeds. For hours he sat in the sun, wearing a floppy hat, straining his tomatoes over a wooden barrel. Not a single seed was permitted in the mixture, and I inspected it frequently for quality.

'Signorina, how about a little tea break?' he asked after a while, his eyes glinting with mischief. 'What about a little recreation?'

'Not until you have quite finished, my lazy apprentice,' I answered.

Later, when all the tomatoes were sieved and there was no trace of skin or pips, we added some handfuls of salt and leaves of fragrant basil and poured the entire mixture onto the centre of a large table we had set out in the sun behind the house.

Slowly, over a period of two days during which you must remember to stir frequently, the sun heats the mixture and evaporates the water, leaving a sumptuous, rich, dark tomato paste, which gives our pasta sauces their unique taste.

All day long, for two long days, I made l'Inglese stir the *'strattu* with a large wooden spoon. And as he stirred we talked.

I told him about my family: I described Mama, Papa, and my brothers. He was particularly interested in Guerra and Pace. Dear boys. How I missed them.

I told him about the *fattoria* where I grew up, and described to him in detail *la cucina*, which he never tired of hearing about. He even asked me to draw a diagram so he could understand the layout more clearly.

'Ah, signorina, it reminds me of the kitchen in the house where I spent the summer holidays of my childhood. In Provence. It is there that I acquired the love of food, and the pleasure of cooking. Tell me, signorina, why is it you leave such a *cucina* for the closet you call a kitchen here in Palermo?'

'Ah, it is a long story, signor.'

'I have the time, signorina. My instructor tells me I must stir this wretched substance every few seconds for the next two days. She is a tyrant. A positive tyrant. And so I beg you, signorina, begin your story. My hours are at your disposal. I am going nowhere.'

And so, faltering at first, I began to tell my story. He listened with rapt attention as it unfolded, and at times I had to remind him to stir the *'strattu*, for he was so engrossed in my words he forgot everything else. There were times when I was sure I saw tears well up in his blue eyes, and then he would grasp my hand with his in a gesture of sympathy and understanding.

It was the first time I had ever spoken of my past, and yet it felt right to reveal my secret to this man, on that day, that summer, under the burning sun.

When I had finished my story I felt free and light. I had told it as it was, and it was laid out between us like

the planks of a bridge. It felt so good to trust him and be
open to him and let him into my world.

'What an incredible story, signorina,' he said after a
pause, which he had filled with much stirring of the
'strattu.

'I knew the instant I set my eyes upon you that you
had a secret, a sadness which showed in the shadows
behind your eyes, even when you smiled, but my guesses
were poor bloodless creatures. How I hoped you would
share it with me. You are an amazing woman, Rosa
Fiore. All my life I have been looking for someone like
you. We are two of a kind, you and I. Kindred spirits.'

'But how can you know that,' I asked, 'when we know
each other so little?'

'Oh, signorina, how much you have to learn. A thing
between a man and a woman is not based on the length
of time they have known each other, or on their knowledge of the other's chronology, their place of birth, what
they do, or whether or not they like cats.' He gestured
expansively with his wooden spoon, as though searching
for the right words in the air.

'All of that means nothing. It is irrelevant. What brings
a man and a woman together is simply a matter of the
heart. When I saw you for the first time that day in
the library, my heart spoke to yours. Don't pretend you
didn't hear it. And don't be fearful. Live it. Enjoy it.'

'I know you are right. But it feels so strange. So fast.
So incredible.'

'It's wonderful, isn't it?' he said, kissing me.

I had to agree: it was wonderful.

As night fell we set the *'strattu* on the porch to keep it

free of dew which would make it moist again and spoil it. Then together we prepared a magnificent *tonno alla Siracusa*, fresh from the sea.

I showed l'Inglese how to slice little incisions in the fragrant flesh of the fish and fill them with a mixture of crushed garlic, cloves, and coriander. I loved the way he wielded a knife with the flamboyant gestures of his beautiful hands. Everything this man did with his hands had me fascinated.

Once the fish was well stuffed with the garlic mixture, we added it to the pan containing the onions we had already softened. Tomatoes, white wine vinegar, and oregano were added next, and while the dish cooked it filled the air with a sumptuous aroma of garlic, herbs, and wine. This heady cocktail stimulated the passions of the hungry and impatient cooks.

'You will notice how much more delicious the food tastes after making love, signorina,' said l'Inglese, still lying naked on the flagstone floor of the kitchen, wafting a cigarette between his fingers, while I checked the pans and tried to find my dress, which had somehow got lost in the scramble and urgency of the moment.

He was right, of course. The *tonno alla Siracusa* was the finest I had ever tasted. When I close my eyes now and think about it, I can still recall the taste of the fish that night and my mouth waters.

Finally, at the end of the second day, when the *'strattu* had reached the right consistency, like thick, dry mud, I showed l'Inglese how to pack it tightly into jars and cover it with oil and salt and a layer of muslin. If wrapped carefully, it will last right through the winter. It gave me such joy to see those jars lined up on the shelf in the kitchen; it was like being home once more.

When we subsequently sat down to a mountain of *pasta con acciughe e mollica* made with the paste, l'Inglese had to admit that all the effort had been worth it: he had never tasted a sauce so delicious.

CHAPTER SIX

I spent all my spare time with l'Inglese, teaching him
about the kitchen, and he in turn taught me the secrets of
the bedroom. Still, I did not neglect my duties at the
library.

One evening, towards the end of July, always an
unbearably sticky month in Palermo, I was on late duty,
and was alone in the library save for Crocifisso the
doorman. He was listening to the commentary of a foot-
ball match on a transistor radio in his little booth.

There were no readers at all in the library. The university students were on vacation, and the regulars had
already gone home. It was quiet, just as I liked it, and I
was able to get on with some shelving in peace. Sometimes it pleased me to help the junior girls by doing this:
after all, this was how I had started.

L'Inglese had gone out of town for a few days, on
business, he said, although I didn't know what business.
When I asked, he assumed an air of mystery and said he
would tell me when he came back. I was not really very
curious: although I would miss him, his absence meant I

would be able to get on and do a few things in my apartment that I had been putting off. Putting things off was not something I liked to do.

I was so happy as I pushed my little cart between the shelves, filing each of the books away according to the catalogue numbers that I had assigned to them.

How my life had changed since l'Inglese had appeared in it, I mused as I refilled my cart with a stack of returned items. What wonderful times we had had together over the past few magical weeks. I hoped it would never end.

Sandwiched between the high rows of medical books on the second floor I suddenly had the feeling I was being watched. It was the same feeling I had had in my apartment when Signor Rivoli was leering at me from his balcony. A shiver that started between my shoulder blades rippled its way through the length of my body. The light up in that part of the library was not too good. I looked all around me, and then walked gingerly between the rows, looking and listening. But there was no-one there; I was just being foolish.

I returned to my cart and continued with my duties. Then I picked up a book, a much-thumbed volume on human reproduction, and found a piece of paper inserted between two pages. I removed it, as was my custom, and found on it a little drawing of two figures locked in an embrace. The male figure had a little moustache, a large paunch, and a monstrous phallus. The female figure had huge breasts and in every other detail looked very much like me. On the reverse, in his calligraphic script, l'Inglese had written 'I miss you.' I smiled broadly as I put it away in my pocket. How had he managed to plant the note so that only I would find it? He was a constant source of delight to me. I loved these little gestures: no-one had ever tried to please me before, and I lapped it up.

Suddenly, while I was lost in thought, I felt a shadow pass swiftly between me and the light. I shivered again. There was nobody there, I had checked. What was the matter with me this evening? Nerves, that was all. I promised myself that as soon as I reached my apartment I would take a comforting bath followed by a dish of fried calves' brains. That was sure to cure me of these jitters.

I decided to stop work there and then and leave the library. Crocifisso would make sure everything was secure. I had finished most of the shelving: there was only one stack left for the girls in the morning. I almost ran down the huge staircase that hugged the stone walls of the central hall. I had never felt like this in the library before. Despite my air of assumed composure I felt very uneasy indeed.

I could hear the sports commentator's voice rising with excitement as one of the teams scored a goal. It was a comfort to hear the noise of normal life going on. I was foolish to be frightened.

'Good night, Crocifisso,' I called as I headed for the door, 'I'm finishing a little early.' There came no reply.

'Good night!' I shouted louder, thinking he could not hear me over the sound of the transistor.

I walked over to his little booth, but to my surprise it was empty. I waited for a few moments, thinking he had gone to the lavatory, but he did not reappear. This was strange: he did not usually begin his rounds of the building so early.

I felt I could not go without speaking to him, so I waited. Ten minutes passed. I switched off the transistor and strained my ears for the sound of his footsteps in the echoing corridors. There was no noise, just the regular ticking of the great clock, like a giant's heartbeat. What should I do?

I did not allow myself to feel the fear that was welling up inside me. But I knew that something was very wrong. The library did not feel right that night; the warm and kindly feeling of the grand old place had somehow gone. I had never, in twenty-five years of working there, ever felt frightened before. Goose bumps hung on my body like water did after *la doccia*. I could not shake them off.

I walked through the ground floor corridors calling for Crocifisso. My footsteps clattered eerily on the tiles. The air had become thick. There was no trace of Crocifisso, but I found one of the fire doors into the rear alley open. This was not right at all. The alley was in darkness now: it was almost nine o'clock. Was there anyone there? I peered out into the darkness but could see nothing. All the usual night-time noise of Palermo sounded strangely far off. Had anyone come inside? Perhaps Crocifisso was in danger. Perhaps while I had been wasting time he had been engaged in a bloody struggle with an intruder.

I ran back to the front office. I would use the telephone to call the police. Yes, of course, that's what I would do. I grabbed the receiver but there was no sound: the telephone lines were out. I could feel a ball of fear in my stomach. I had to help Crocifisso. Where was he? I ran up the stairs to the upper floors and quickly scanned the chambers and corridors. There was no sign of any disturbance or anything unusual.

The basement. The thought of the basement came to me with a lurch. I would have to go down there. It would have to be the basement. In films, horrible things always happen in basements.

I slithered down the spiral staircase, almost missing my footing in the haste to propel my body forward before its natural reluctance would apply the brakes. The lights were off. I knew the basement so well that I quickly found the switch, even in the darkness. Only a loud irregular breathing broke the silence. I realized it was my own. As the lights came up I was afraid of what I might see.

'Crocifisso,' I called. 'Are you down here? Are you all right? Answer me.'

It must have been instinct that guided me towards the section housing the first editions. The precious works were kept in display cases, tables with glass covers protecting the pages from dust and greasy fingers.

My feet walked me towards one of the display cases. From a distance I could see it had been disturbed. I noticed my cheeks were wet. I was crying. There was something wrong with the glass case. Very wrong. There was something in it that should not have been there. I rubbed my eyes to clear away the tears that were blurring everything. There was a form in there. It looked like a human form. A body. Someone's body. Crocifisso's body. I knew immediately and instinctively that he was dead. Anyone who has ever seen a dead body will agree that it has a look of its own. The display case had become a glass-topped coffin. I looked down at his face, at Crocifisso's face. I touched the glass over his face with my fingers. My tears dripped onto it.

CHAPTER SEVEN

The body was removed from the glass case and taken
away in an ambulance to the mortuary. The blade of a
knife had sliced through Crocifisso's heart. As a result,
the first editions were badly stained with blood and I
could not clean them.

I thought the police would want to ask me lots of
questions, but they had no interest in me at all and, if
anything, treated my attempts to explain what little I
knew as a nuisance. None of them would listen to me.
Finally, in frustration, I approached a man who seemed
to be senior to the others. I was sure I had seen his face
somewhere before, but I could not place him.

'I found the body, signor,' I said. 'Shouldn't I tell
someone about it?'

'Look, signora,' he said, 'there are a hundred murders a
week in this city. What makes you think this one is
special?'

Poor Crocifisso, even in death he was a nobody. Before
I left the library I went into his booth to collect his few
possessions to return to his wife. How would she manage

now? In his desk drawer I found the tin of *nucatoli* I had made for his children and given him earlier that day to take home. I packed them with his transistor radio, a few personal items, and his cap into a box. I would deliver them tomorrow.

As I came out into the street I saw a familiar figure in the shadows heading towards the Piazza Bologni. I recognized the figure. The height was right. The build – a little stocky – the walk, the clothes. Surely it was l'Inglese. What was he doing here? He was supposed to be away on business until Friday. What did this mean? Had he not gone away after all? It was very strange. I had to catch up with him and find out what was going on.

I crossed the Via Vittoria Emanuele and followed him. He was walking fast. I couldn't allow myself to lose sight of him. He was at a distance too far to hear me call out to him. I marched as quickly as I could, trying to reach him.

He cut down between La Martorana and San Nicolo and on through the narrow streets towards La Cala.

My heart was thumping in my breast from the exertion, making me feel nauseous, but I had to catch him. The adrenalin kept me going. I had to know what this meant. Why was he in Palermo now when he was supposed to be away?

Had he lied to me? If he had lied about this, had he lied about other things? Suspicion ran along beside me, encouraging me. Had his whole story been a tissue of lies?

I would catch him. I would force the truth out of him. I would look him in the eye and ask him what all this meant. He was outpacing me. I had to run faster. How my lungs burned.

Now, after one final burst of effort, I was closing in on him. Why did he not turn around at the sound of my footsteps? From the Via Alloro he cut through into the Via Scopari and disappeared into a doorway. There was a steep staircase leading down to a bar in the basement. I hurried down without hesitation. I would catch him now. I had to know the truth.

I threw open the door, panting. L'Inglese was at the bar ordering a drink. He turned round to face me. Only it was someone else. It was not l'Inglese at all. What a fool I looked, standing puffing in the doorway like a steam train. The sailors standing around and drinking laughed at me.

'Are you all right, Mother?' they asked cheekily.

I hurried out again and staggered up the staircase. What a fool you are, Rosa Fiore, I said to myself. I burned with embarrassment.

But then I felt a sudden joy. It was not him. It was not him. He was not here. He had gone away. He had not lied to me. It was all right. Everything was as it had been before. He was honest and good, and I had been wicked to doubt him. I had no reason to doubt him. I was just being stupid. He was wonderful and I loved him. I was just overwrought: a murder is never good for the nerves. I needed to get home and fry those brains and calm myself. I was so relieved.

I walked slowly along the Via Vittorio Emanuele, the most direct and safest route to my apartment. I could not rush any more. My chase of the wrong man had left me close to collapse. Having crossed the Quattro Canti I walked on past the library. All was quiet. Poor Crocifisso.

At last I reached my apartment and immediately lit the gas stove. I warmed some oil in a pan and sliced some bread. Why would anyone want to kill Crocifisso? He was the doorman at the public library, of interest to no-one. I unwrapped the bloodied paper packet of brains. No brains are as sweet as those of a baby cow. I felt them with my fingers. How cool and soft and tantalizing. I dropped them in pink clusters into the hot oil. They spat.

I suppose the policeman, if that is what he was, was right. In this city murders were not remarkable. There did not even have to be a reason. Though of course that would be scant consolation to the man's wife and seven children.

I sandwiched the brains between the slices of bread and bit into them hungrily. A simple dish, but succulent. Only then, when my stomach was full of food, did the horrors of the day begin to recede, and I was able to find a little peace.

CHAPTER EIGHT

The library felt awful after Crocifisso's death. It was as though the old place were shocked at what it had witnessed.

The regular readers were in a state of deep sorrow. Many had known Crocifisso since he joined the library, just out of military service, back in the late twenties. They had danced at his wedding; they were godfathers to his children. Now they were to carry him to his final resting place. The old men sat and talked for hours on end trying to understand it. They asked the same question: why? why? why?

The library assistants did not stop crying for days. No work was done as they spent all their time huddled together consoling one another. The egoist Costanza became subject to bizarre fainting fits, which could only be cured by a lengthy spell lying down on the couch in the director's office. Soon disorder was finding its way onto the shelves: books were replaced in the wrong places, catalogue cards went missing. I had to work extra hours to put things right.

There were still three days to go until l'Inglese's return: I was counting the hours. I ached to have him hold me in his arms as tightly as he could. Only that would make the pain go away.

We still had the funeral to get through. The entire library community attended. We went together in a line led by the director to the little church of Santa Maria del Spasimo, over near the Botanical Gardens.

Signora Rossi, Crocifisso's wife, had to be held up by her neighbours. The seven *bambini* were lined up in order of size next to the coffin, which had to be paid for by subscription. Although it was not lavish, we did our best to give him an honourable send-off. I was surprised to see the police inspector and one of his colleagues hovering by the cemetery gates. I knew that man from somewhere, but where?

Afterwards we returned to the Rossis' one-room apartment in the Via Rocco Pirri. I had prepared some food for the mourners: a large *sfincione*, some cured ham, and *mustazzoli* cookies to follow. The *bambini* ate hurriedly; it seemed *la signora* had forgotten to feed them since the tragedy. She sat in a corner with a look of complete despair in her eyes. No-one could reach her, not even the *bambini* who tugged in vain at her skirts. The library assistants made such a din with their wailing that the director had to send them all home.

Following the funeral, we all made an effort to try and return to a semblance of normality. The director held a staff meeting and told the library assistants that although we were all distraught over Crocifisso's death and the manner in which it had taken place, we could not allow standards to slip, and we had to apply ourselves to our duties. There was redemption in work, and while we were carrying out our given tasks, we were honouring Crocifisso's memory.

The director also took this opportunity to introduce the new doorman, the one-eyed Restituto Raimondo, whom we should welcome with warm hearts into our midst.

Restituto Raimondo bowed. He bore the mark of the desperation that had forced him to take a murdered man's job.

At last Friday came and l'Inglese returned. I was so hungry for comfort I almost squeezed the breath from his body. Between sobs, I recounted to him the events of the past few days, and he held me tight and let me cry myself calm.

'It's all right, old girl,' he said, rocking me back and forth. 'I'm back now. Everything is going to be all right.'

'Is it?' I asked, my eyes blurry with tears.

'Yes, it is.'

This was just what my soul hungered to hear.

That night l'Inglese was so gentle in his lovemaking that for the first time I experienced what a comfort sex could be to a tired and troubled mind. Up until now I had only experienced this solace through my labours in the kitchen.

Afterwards, as he held me close, I asked what business it was that had called him away.

'Rosa, don't ask me. It's better that you don't know.'

'Better for whom? It's not better for me. I hate not knowing anything about you.'

'But Rosa, you know everything about me. Everything

that it is important to know. All the rest is nothing. It's not important. What we have between us is everything.'

'But what do we have? I'm not sure. It scares me sometimes.'

'We have each other, of course. A horrible thing has happened, I know. And I'm sorry I wasn't here to help you. But don't start fretting about everything else. Don't look for things to worry about. Rosa, I love you.'

'Do you?' I asked, incredulously.

'Of course I do. Couldn't you tell?'

'I wasn't sure.'

'Well, I do. Do you love me?'

'It's hard to love someone you don't know anything about. What was it that called you away?'

'I can't tell you that. Not just yet. For your own safety. But when this is over, I promise, I'll tell you everything. And then we'll see if you love me or not.'

'When what is over?'

'I can't tell you. Don't make me lie to you. Please don't ask me any more questions. Just trust me. You do trust me, don't you?'

'Yes, I trust you,' I said, although I was not entirely convinced that I did.

L'Inglese soon fell into a sweet deep sleep, while I lay awake thinking. Grudgingly, I had to accept this mystery, for now at least. It was not until much later that I learned the men who had murdered Crocifisso had in fact been looking for l'Inglese himself.

CHAPTER NINE

It was a perfect end-of-summer evening. For a long time the huge red sun had perched on the edge of the sea before, in an instant, dropping down out of sight. It was the kind of evening that stays hot even after the sun has gone down, and all around objects retain a rosy glow absorbed during the day from the sun's rays.

I was wandering barefoot in the gardens of l'Inglese's villa at Acquasanta. I was filled with joy, an all-consuming feeling of the utmost pleasure that rolled around inside me, filling all my empty spaces.

Inside the house, l'Inglese was preparing supper. Tonight he was going to cook for me; he had been making preparations all day, and would not allow me into the kitchen. I love surprises, and anticipated our meal with a deep-seated excitement. I knew this man was incapable of disappointing me; he was equally incapable of doing the expected. If I had learned anything about him over the past few weeks it was that he was always completely unpredictable.

Oh, what a summer we'd had. It was as if my whole

life was a mere dress rehearsal for this moment. How I had changed over the last few weeks. From the dull spinster librarian I had suddenly turned into a woman, a real woman.

The staff in the library couldn't believe it; even Costanza had stopped laughing at me. In fact, she now regarded me with awe. She knew the truth, that she herself could not manage such a man; he frightened her despite her bravado with the opposite sex. He was a man who would not play games.

For the first time in my life I was completely happy. I had the feeling that if I were to die tomorrow I would be satisfied with my life; I had known what it was to experience life and to experience love.

The marble walkways of the garden were still warm from the sun and felt slightly chalky under the soles of my bare feet. Just a few weeks ago I had been leading a sort of half-life, a life with the light switched off, a life of half-darkness; now I was open to every new experience: the feel of the stone beneath my feet, the colour and the smell of the sea, the caress of the breeze on my cheek, the texture of the air against my skin. I breathed deeply, as if inhaling the world anew: dew, the sound of far-off laughter, the tinkling of fountains, cool water, distant bells slightly flat in tone, children playing, the birds singing and the insects buzzing, the cicadas in the leaves, a large dog barking in the distance, and far, far away the rumble of the railway, the pattern of shadows through the palm fronds, the fleeting glimpse of a lizard against a white wall before its shadow grazed past the corner of the eye.

The garden at Acquasanta was the nearest place to paradise that I had ever seen. Well-trimmed palm trees and sweet-smelling pines were interspersed with fruit trees bearing oranges, lemons, grapefruit, and kumquats. The branches bowed down under the weight of the golden fruit.

Low box hedges bordered the flower gardens. There were cornflowers and sweet peas and arum lilies. Terracotta pots the size of men trailed trains of ivy and overflowed with pink geraniums.

As I wandered through the walkways I felt that I was living someone else's life; could this really be happening to Rosa Fiore? I looked down into the well, its yellow stone walls clad in rambling roses. I called out my name. The well echoed back, calling, 'Rooooooooosa, Rooooooooosa.'

'Rooooosa!' Someone else was calling me; it was l'Inglese, bringing me a glass of wine. He was wearing a shirt, a pair of greasy espadrilles, and a broad-brimmed hat. Nothing else.

'Are you all right out here, my Rosa?'

'Yes, I'm fine, really. It's so beautiful here.'

'I won't be too much longer.'

He kissed me, feeling my tongue with his, deeply, softly, before trotting back to his kitchen with a bulge distorting the line of his shirt.

I could never have imagined feeling so at ease with another person. I loved everything about him. Most of all I loved his daring: his bravura, his wildness, the way he did not care about convention, or what people thought of him. He was a free man, free to be himself. I think this is what first spoke to me in him: it felt at first like danger, but it was more than that, something deeper; it was a voice that spoke to me of freedom, giving me courage, for the first time, to be myself.

I loved his warmth, his passion, his hunger for life, his exuberance. Life with him was a constantly expanding adventure, and I was learning from him all the time.

Physically I loved his smell, his breath, his warm soft body, the wonderful things his body did to my body, the way he made me feel like a princess, the way he made me laugh. He had changed my life.

I did not realize at the time just how much I did not know about him. Being so totally immersed in him, I could not look at him with any degree of objectivity. The eye cannot properly see things that are too close: newsprint becomes a blur of black stripes on white, colours merge into one another, features become distorted and hideous. I was caught up in the business of living, like a paper is snatched up in a gust of wind; it is blown up to the rooftops and floats giddily around before plunging back down to the street below.

Wandering among the banks of marigolds, I inhaled the salty scent of the sea. The slight breeze ruffled the hair of the palms and tickled the clusters of laburnum draped over the walls.

Out beyond the safety of the harbour a tiny fishing boat bobbed up and down, its little gaslight illuminating the gathering inkiness. The sky was indistinguishable from the sea.

As I watched the lonely little boat, l'Inglese came up behind me and circled me in his arms; I nestled into him.

'Everything is ready for your pleasure, Signorina Fiore, if you please come into the house.'

We walked in with our arms around each other.

Inside, he had transformed the kitchen into a magical grotto. Everywhere there were flickering candles and vases of lilies exhaling their intoxicating scent. The various aromas escaping from the pans on the stove stirred my own juices: my taste buds and my loins both began to water.

'Now, my love,' said l'Inglese, 'while I make the very final touches I want you to take your clothes off.'

I felt a hunching of sinews deep down inside me as I began to undress. Slowly, provocatively, I undid the buttons of my dress and slipped it off. I could feel his blue eyes on me as I peeled off my slip, the static crackling and drawing my hair up on end behind it. I had left off my corset since that night when l'Inglese had been forced to cut me out of it. I felt resplendent and not the least bit embarrassed. My nipples stood up huge and hard in their excitement and a silvery liquid slipped gently down my inner thighs.

I started caressing him in the ways he loved. My touch was like that of an angel playing its harp, he had told me.

'Rosa, you mustn't interfere with me while I'm cooking: it spoils my concentration. Now you go and get onto the table. I'll be right there.'

It is impossible to say whether the ripe aroma of sex or the scents of baking bread, melting cheese, roasting flesh, and garlic dominated the air.

I climbed on a chair and then onto the table.

There I lay, luxuriantly, the cool silky oak sticking to

my naked flesh. Rump, thighs, plump. This night was the culmination, the final lesson. By the light of the candles I stretched out and watched l'Inglese as he moved gently among the shadows on the far side of the kitchen, the clattering of his pans punctuated occasionally by the sounds of the summer night, the buzzing of a mosquito, the braying of a mule.

At last everything was ready and l'Inglese approached with the antipasto, a salver bearing plump oysters. I noticed that he had removed his shirt and was now as naked as I. Carefully he tucked a little pillow under my head and then began to place the oysters on my body. They were soft, cool, moist, slimy on my naked flesh. Oh, it was the most wonderful, the most sensuous feeling I have ever experienced.

He arranged them on my throat, around and between my full breasts, on my curved stomach, and on the little thatch of my pubis. He tucked several in between my legs, and others at regular intervals along my thighs, knees and calves. I found it very difficult to keep still. The moment was so erotic that I was on the verge of orgasm already.

L'Inglese stood back with half-closed eyes to get an overall view of his arrangement, and made a little adjustment here and there in the spacing of the oysters on his living platter. Finally, satisfied, he sucked up the first oyster from my foot. I felt his whiskers brush my skin, and the combination of this bristliness with the oyster's slimy softness was so exquisite that I lurched and nearly dislodged everything.

Holding it between his lips, he placed it in my mouth.

It tasted of the sea, the salty blue-green depths. I swallowed and felt it ooze into my throat, filling it, before slipping silkily away.

Now l'Inglese climbed onto the table and drew into his mouth the oysters with which he had clothed me, alternately feeding me and then himself, and moving up along my body. My excitement was so intense that I was almost delirious; I felt as though I was drowning in a sea of honey that filled my every space, engulfing me totally.

L'Inglese's magnificent member brushed against my electric flesh and I gasped out loud, yearning to satisfy this agony of expectation and desire. But still he fed me and fed off me, slowly and deliberately.

Finally all the oysters had been swallowed and I was limp and weak and full of yearning. Carefully l'Inglese wiped me down with a napkin bathed in ice water to eradicate the fishy odours. I produced so much lubricant that it was dripping from the edge of the table, and still it continued to gush, sending rivulets of silver onto the floor.

During the brief lull while l'Inglese adjusted the seasoning of *il primo*, my mind wandered to my colleagues at the library: the director, the hussy Costanza, and the other library assistants. What would they think if they could see me now, the frigid spinster, the laughable virgin Signorina Fiore, lying naked on l'Inglese's table while he ate his food from the folds of her flesh? What would the interfering Nonna Frolla think, or my neighbours in the apartment building on the Via Vicolo Brugno, or indeed the perverted Signor Rivoli? I smiled at the thought of their moral outrage and at the thought of my wonderful secret life. I had always loved secrets.

In the midst of my reflections the pasta appeared. L'Inglese had evidently paid attention to my lessons in the kitchen and had managed to make his own spaghetti. Admittedly, it was not as fine as my own, but nevertheless he had taken a great deal of time and care over it.

He had produced a marvellous ragù with meat, tomatoes, and lots of garlic. As I watched, he mixed in the sauce with the spaghetti. After making sure it wasn't too hot, he ladled it onto my body. What a mess it made. It was everywhere, covering my ample body's entire surface. Then, climbing astride me, he began to take up the spaghetti in long strings into his mouth, sucking it in, so that he too quickly became covered in the rich sauce. It was clinging to his moustache, his chin, his chest, his stomach, his legs. With his hands, he fed the spaghetti to me, trailing its tendrils between my parted lips. It was divine. Mmmmmm. A truly wonderful sauce; lots of garlic, tender chunks of meat.

'Is it all right?' he asked shyly.

'It's wonderful, it really is.'

It felt lovely; both of us bathed in it. I sucked greedily at the spaghetti. He wove it into my hair. It got into my ears, my eyes, everywhere.

Finally, when we had licked each other clean of the sauce, we vowed we would never eat spaghetti from a plate again. How much better it tasted like this.

And so we continued with *il secondo*, tender young veal in a sauce of wild mushrooms, served with spinach and baby peas. This time I insisted that l'Inglese be the one to lie on the table. I sliced the meat into bite-sized chunks and arranged them over his belly and crotch.

How I delighted in snatching up with my teeth the sweet morsels of veal and the plump field mushrooms. I loved to eat off him, nuzzling into him with my nose, lapping up every drop of the delicious sauce filling his navel and the folds of his groin. I sucked up the sauce from his penis, causing it to spring up with a jolt as though it had experienced an electric shock. Now it was his turn to moan and groan as I teased him with my tongue.

For dessert he smeared my breasts with gelati and a sauce of raspberries. Ooooh, it was cold! As a garnish he placed individual raspberries in the mounds of ice cream so that it looked as though I had many nipples, and it was impossible to tell which were the real ones and which were not. L'Inglese took his revenge for the anxiety I caused him with my lusty nips at the veal chunks. He made snarling noises and bit savagely into the raspberries, making me squeal.

After the meal was finally over, he lowered himself into me and the yearning of the past two teasing hours on the table was satisfied at last.

And so we had both learned our lessons: l'Inglese had become skilled in the arts of the Sicilian kitchen, and I, the librarian, had learned what it is to love and be loved by a man. What a banquet of the senses it had been.

L'Autunno

THE AUTUMN

CHAPTER ONE

It was now the end of summer.

A special between-time follows. In any one year it lasts at most two or three days. In that brief interval it is no longer summer and not yet autumn. The air loses its softness, like a once-fluffy bath towel that has been too many times to the laundry. The days are still hot but the nights become cooler, and in the morning there is a slight sadness in the heart for the long hot days that will soon be over.

It was a Saturday afternoon. I was walking out to l'Inglese's villa in the Via Belmonte. That evening it was my turn to cook. My basket was straining with the weight of beef, salami, tomatoes, caciocavallo and pecorino cheeses, raisins, pine nuts, and onions.

I was going to make a *braciolettine* for l'Inglese. I knew he would enjoy it.

It was very hot in the afternoon sun, and climbing the hill I started to breathe deeply. I could feel the pulse twitching at the nape of my neck, and smell the heat of my body rising between my breasts. A trickle

187

of sweat began to trace its way down my spine.

My labouring heartbeat was the only sound. The city was sleeping. Soon I would be naked, splayed out like a precious butterfly on the crisp linen sheets of l'Inglese's bed under the mosquito net and the cooling whirr of the ceiling fan.

Perhaps he would tether my limbs to the bed frame with veils. I liked the idea of being so completely open to him.

Perhaps he would stroke me with a white feather starting at the soles of my feet, tickling me until I squealed.

Perhaps he would blindfold me, enabling me to plunge in the crystal waters of an ocean of sensuous bliss, the waters finding and filling every space in my electric body.

I was already wet inside with anticipation.

I walked up the long gravel drive of the villa. The white house shimmered in the sunshine like a mirage in the desert. My footsteps crunched on the tiny stones. Fleeting lizards shied away; their shadows could not keep pace with them.

The long drive was overhung by dwarf palms, willows, and lemon trees.

There was only silence and heat and the crunch of the gravel and the sound of heat pulsing in my ears.

I expected to see l'Inglese coming out from the house or the gardens to meet me. He ran down the steps sometimes wearing only a shirt and his floppy hat, sometimes wearing only his hat and nothing else, a wide smile, sparkling blue eyes. But he did not come. He hadn't heard me; he was probably preparing something in the kitchen to surprise me. Perhaps he was engrossed in a book or snoozing in his hammock. I planned to surprise him, to creep up to him noiselessly and kiss him gently awake. I would kiss his sleeping eyelids and relaxed mouth; I would take his sleeping willy into my mouth and coax it to life. He would pretend to still be asleep to prolong the wonderful awakening. I smiled to myself.

I climbed the steps and pushed open the door. There was an emptiness in the house that I felt but did not acknowledge then.

'Darling?' I called. My voice echoed through the marble hall.

He had to be in the gardens. I wandered along the gravel walkways overlooking the sea, to the miniature temple on the far side. He was not there.

'He is hiding somewhere,' I thought.

A game of cat and mouse. I would find him before he found me. A frisson of excitement bubbled through me. He was watching me from a hidey-hole somewhere, ready to spring out at me and make me jump. He was hunting me, stalking me. He would lunge at me from behind, unawares, push me to the ground and ravish me. I imagined the gravel indenting irregular shapes on my knees, palms, cheeks, my mouth full of dust, the force of his thrusts, which had the power to make me scream out loud, with no care of being overheard.

I crouched down behind the hydrangeas and scanned through half-closed eyes the sleeping windows of the house. All were shuttered; nothing was visible. I moved stealthily behind the hedges, trying to keep down and out of sight. I moved like this through the rose gardens towards the fountain.

He had not doubled back and sneaked into his hammock. He was not in the lemon grove. He was not in the arbour under the clusters of vines. Where was he?

I circled the house before going inside.

Of course, he was in the bedroom, waiting for me.

'What has taken you so long, signorina?' he would ask. He still called me this sometimes.

I would take him into my mouth and feed on him. Hungrily enjoying the taut, smooth skin, the warmth, the weight, the size, the involuntary spasms, the taste of yogurt, the smell of warmth, the moaning, groaning, wincing pleasure.

I dashed up the stairs and, now out of breath, threw the door open.

He was not there. All was silent. The bed was undisturbed. The clock ticked. His smell lingered in the still air. His cologne, the peppermint freshness, the manness.

He was in the kitchen, obviously, preparing some delicious dish to feed me after our lovemaking had sapped us of all energy, leaving us euphoric and ethereal. Then we were like snails without shells: we were soft and new-formed and felt the world as a new place against our dewy pink skin.

Perhaps he would feed me oysters or caviar; perhaps he would make his wonderful recipe of eggs cooked slowly with butter and chopped chives; or wedges of deep-fried cheese oozing glossy tongues into beds of *lollo rosso* and fingers of toasted bread. Lovers' food, which he would eat off my naked body, his moustache tickling me

190

as he fed me from his own lips with the most succulent morsels. My mouth watered in anticipation of the delights to come.

I ran down the stairs, my legs going almost too fast for my body, through the marble passages to the kitchen. The marvellous kitchen with its long table, the scene of that magical evening when my body became a part of his banquet, our passion for the food melting into our desire for the other's flesh.

And yet he was not there. Where could he be? The copper pans gleamed on their hooks against the walls. A solitary fly zigzagged under the central lamp. There was a smell of burnt sugar and vanilla and I yearned for l'Inglese to touch me. I opened the shutters, admitting the light. From outside came the hum of warmth and insects and sun and heat. How I loved him. Loved him with every nerve in my body. Where was he?

I experienced a sudden panic. For the first time it occurred to me that he had gone; that I might never see him again. I felt a deep pain, as though a large smooth stone was inside my stomach, weighing it down.

But the elasticity of the lover's thoughts is such that I banished from my mind the horrible truth and persuaded myself that he would certainly reappear, and soon.

I retrieved my basket from where I had abandoned it on the front steps and, bringing it into the kitchen, I unloaded the contents onto the table. I would get on with preparing the food, ready for his return.

I fried the onion and, while it was sweating in the pan, I cut the beef round into thin slices. When the onion was soft I removed it from the heat and stirred in the bread crumbs, pecorino cheese, raisins, pine nuts, tomatoes, salt, and pepper. Mixing these ingredients thoroughly together, I then placed a spoonful on each of the beef slices and added a cube of cheese and a chunk of salami. Finally I rolled up the slices of meat, threaded them onto skewers, brushed them with oil, and placed them to cook in the wood-burning stove.

When the meat was cooked it sent a tantalizing aroma into the warm air. Still l'Inglese had not returned. It was now around four and the sun was beginning to lose its fierceness. I wandered out into the garden with a book and gingerly clambered into the hammock. As I lazily turned the pages sleep slowly stole me away. My eyes blinked heavily and closed, and soon the gentle sound of my snores joined the hum of the cicadas and the buzzing of bees.

Much, much later, the cooling of the air roused me from my luxurious dreams of dumplings and fleshy sausages. Goose bumps pricked my arms. A chill passed through my body. It was growing dark. I swung myself down from the hammock and walked up to the house. Inside there was still no sign of l'Inglese. The dish of *braciolettine* was cold and congealed on the table. The copper pans jeered at me, reflecting the hideous mask of my face.

Late into the night I sat and waited. Please come, I thought. Please come and make a mockery of these awful thoughts.

I left the villa after midnight, sadly retracing my steps to the Via Vicolo Brugno, my mind deadened.

The next day, after a sleepless night, I returned to the

192

villa. All of his things were still there. His floppy garden hat and a half-empty packet of cigarettes on the kitchen counter made me crumple and sob for the first time. The cold *braciolettine* was still on the table.

Upstairs, his room remained the same as it had been all those years ago, before everything changed. His books were still piled up by the bed. Among them I found the sheaf of notes he had made that Monday in the manuscript room at the library. The pages were bordered by obscene doodles of figures, which resembled the two of us. I touched them gently with my fingertips, my mind reliving that day when it all began.

His clothes were still hanging in the wardrobe. I buried my face in them, absorbing his smell. His shoes were lined up in pairs, ready to be put on.

I stayed there a long time. All day, and into the night, I sat on the edge of the bed where I had enjoyed such exquisite pleasures, but now they seemed like a dream, a distant memory of another life. Our smell was still on the bedsheets.

I mourned for l'Inglese, for the time we had had together, and for myself: for my true self, which I had become with him, quite suddenly, in a blaze of colour like a butterfly, and which I would never be again.

A vision came into my mind of a day in summer, of the blinding white light of midday that strikes the eye as you emerge from a shady interior. I was back at the *fattoria*, looking over the top of the stable door that opens from *la cucina* onto the yard. I was wiping some flour from my hands onto the skirt of my apron. Somewhere in the background was the sound of children's voices. In the glare I struggled to identify a figure standing at the gate. A late summer wasp buzzed angrily in my face, jolting me back into reality and the lonely truth of l'Inglese's disappearance.

The following day I came again to the villa. This time I found it all locked up. I could not find a single door open to get inside.

Suddenly autumn had come into the gardens. The flowers had wilted and dropped their heads, scattering petals onto the walkways. The fountain no longer played; it had been boarded up for the winter. Grapes rotted on the vines, feeding swarms of fruit flies that rose up in clouds as I walked by. The hammock had gone. Everywhere there was an air of decay and sadness.

I left the villa knowing that I would never see it again. I knew instinctively that that phase of my life was over.

CHAPTER TWO

I wandered the streets the same way I had done on the first day I came to Palermo. Then I mourned the loss of Bartolomeo; now I mourned the loss of myself.

Eventually I returned, through no conscious will of my own, to my little apartment in the Via Vicolo Brugno. Almost like an automaton I went into the kitchen and began to prepare a comforting *sfincione*. This is the same dish that my mother was preparing at the time of my birth.

I switched on the oven to heat, then dissolved some yeast in a little tepid water and left it to ferment until a froth formed on the surface. The yeasty smell was like that of l'Inglese's skin after we had made love. It filled my nostrils, and closing my eyes I could almost make believe that I was back in his arms, as we lay tangled in a heap after loving one another.

Rousing myself from my reverie, I poured the yeasty froth into the well I had formed in a pile of flour mixed with salt. Then I kneaded. Oh, how kneading still had the power to soothe my soul like nothing else could. Thump,

thump, thump, thump. Pound, pound, pound. Pulse at the temples, sweat beading down the spine. How good this felt. I continued pounding at the dough for a long, long time, until I felt weak, and my anger had, temporarily, diminished.

Then I incorporated a little olive oil into the dough before rolling it into a rectangle and covering it with diced caciocavallo cheese, anchovy fillets, *passata*, and eye-stinging onions. It felt good to cry with the onion vapours; they lent legitimacy to my outpourings of grief. Wiping my nose on the back of my hand and sniffing loudly, I mixed some two-day-old bread crumbs with some crushed oregano leaves I kept hanging in a little bunch by the window, and sprinkled them over the top of the *sfincione*.

Finally I drizzled over some more olive oil and left it to rise for an hour in the warmth of the kitchen, during which time, miraculously, l'Inglese returned.

He had simply been out of town for a few days, on business, and had no way of contacting me. He clearly had not changed his clothes in the time he had been away; they were stained with grime and sweat. He had not shaved either, and the three days' growth of stubble lent him the rakish air of a man who breaks the rules. His eyes were red; he had obviously been drinking hard, and they were hungry, for me, for not having to pretend any more, for the fundamental understanding between a man and a woman.

I inhaled his irresistible aroma, the scent of a fully aroused man; strong, musky, unmistakable. He was ready for me, there was no doubt of that. God, I had missed him. I wanted him so much I was throbbing.

Picking me up in his arms as if I weighed no more than a suckling pig, he kissed me fiercely; his breath a witch's brew of whisky and tobacco. Then he threw me onto the table so that my head landed in the rising *sfincione*, which cushioned it like a pillow. He ripped off my brightly coloured apron, my tight pink blouse and brown skirt, but he did not have time to remove my stockings and my little high-heeled shoes.

Standing erect at the end of the table, he pulled me towards him. I screamed so loudly that the whole neighbourhood heard me. It is said that even the vespers then being conducted in the duomo were halted by the cry.

Nonna Frolla, the pug, her husband, the regular customers at the grocery shop, and the other tenants of the apartment building all ran forth and gathered in the corridor outside my apartment, deliberating as to whether they should force entry. Signor Rivoli was fantasizing about doing precisely that, and from his living room across the street was enjoying this unexpected upturn in my fortune while he masturbated on the carpet.

This time it was l'Inglese's turn to bay like a wolf as I gripped him with my muscles and squeezed him and squeezed him again. The assembled crowd responded with a shout of encouragement – all except Nonna Frolla, who sniffed with a prudish air she did not feel, while the pug, Nero, uttered a sound for the first time in its life. It was not exactly a bark; no, it would not be accurate to describe the sound made by the pug at this juncture as a bark, but nevertheless it was a sound that proved that he too was all too fully aware of the events then taking place inside the librarian's apartment, and this earned him the grudging respect of some of the onlookers, who had, up until now, regarded him as nothing more than an ornament.

The climax was a long time coming. Despite the enormous longing we felt for each other at our long-awaited and very poignant reunion, we managed to continue our lovemaking far into the night. There were the inevitable lulls, times when the tide seemed to ebb slightly before crashing onto the rocks with renewed force, during which the crowd grew restless, but the highs were so high as to be an education for all those gathered in the corridor.

There were, indeed, occasions when the crowd thinned as those who waited there felt themselves swept up in the excitement of the moment, and disappeared for their own bite of the cherry. Strange couplings took place as the urge struck and new friendships were formed.

Quinto Cavallo, the goldsmith from the Via d'Oro, got together with the draper's assistant, Paula Chiacchierone, and the pair disappeared into the communal bathroom; some time later an ugly scene ensued as Signor Placido, in his customary urgency to pee, tried to gain entry by setting his heavy shoulder to the door.

Nonno Frolla himself succumbed to temptation and was discovered by his wife sharing a close embrace with the widow Palumbo in a darkened stairwell. The tensions in the apartment building that day brought about by our reunion took a long time to heal; for the first time in almost a century Nonna Frolla took the decision to deny her husband his Tuesday night rights; and for months afterwards neighbours were at war with one another.

Only when the fire engine came to a screeching halt outside did anyone notice that black smoke was seeping out from under my door. In the ensuing panic to evacuate the building, the pug Nero was trampled fatally underfoot; Signor Placido got his bulk stuck in the stairwell, causing a blockage that could only be released by the strategic application of all available hands to his person. Once the pressure eased it was like a torrent of water breaking through a dam as the residents surged coughing and spluttering into the open air of the street. Nonna Frolla herself broke a leg in the crush, trying to save the pug. She was subsequently carried away on a stretcher in an agony of grief and pain as the little broken form of Nero was tossed down from a broken window. It lay for a long time in the gutter with its four little stiffened legs pointing up until someone threw it into a rubbish bin.

The onlookers and residents gathered outside in the Via Vicolo Brugno could now see smoke escaping from the windows of my apartment. As the firemen smoked cigarettes and played their hoses against the windows of the upper floor, Quinto Cavallo and his newfound sweetheart, Paula Chiacchierone, staggered naked and dazed from the building to a round of applause from the crowd.

'Where is Rosa?' cried Quinto, seeking to shield his modesty from the general view behind cupped hands.

'Rosa! Where is Rosa?' went round the cry.

'She's in there still!' they shouted to the officers of the fire brigade.

'Get her out. You must get her out.'

'Do something!'

'Quickly. Quickly.'

'You've got to get her out. She's in there with that Inglese. They could be dead by now.'

The burliest and bravest of the firemen stormed the building, choking in the thick black fumes as they made their way up the staircase to my apartment. The crowd went suddenly silent. How could we be inside after all this time and still be alive? The chances were small, it had to be said. All stood silent, imagining the charred corpses of the lovers still in flagrante amid the raging inferno. Still, that is the price exacted for an immoral way of life. The headlines of *L'Ora* the following morning would read LASCIVIOUS LIBRARIAN DIES IN LOVE-NEST INFERNO. It was a judgement; that much was clear.

Wait, though, just a second, the firemen were stumbling from the building bearing a stocky figure between them in their arms. They laid it gently down on the pavement. It appeared to be lifeless. One of the firemen knelt down and delivered the kiss of life. There had to be some hope then. Whoever it was was not dead yet. The crowd strained forward, craning their necks to see beyond the huddle of firemen gathered all around.

'It must be Rosa,' the crowd muttered.

It certainly looked like me.

The figure began to convulse and cough and spit and splutter. It was me and I was alive. A cheer broke out among the onlookers as I was placed on a stretcher and carried to an ambulance bound for the infirmary.

'But what about l'Inglese?' asked Quinto Cavallo, who by this stage had managed to borrow a pair of trousers, albeit a rather short pair that barely covered his knees, and a threadbare shirt.

'There was no-one else in there,' replied the chief fire officer, his face blackened with the smoke.

'But of course there was. Her lover, the Inglese. We heard them in there. Up to all sorts of things they were.'

'Signor, we looked everywhere. There was no-one else in the apartment. She was alone in the kitchen. The oven caught fire. There was certainly no man with her; if there was we would have found him. There was only her, and the charred remains of a parrot, burnt alive in its cage.'

'Well, fancy that,' said Quinto, rubbing his head in confusion.

The other residents too could not believe it.

'What happened to him then?' asked one.

'He certainly didn't come out while we were up there,' replied another.

'No, of course he didn't. If he had come out we would have seen him.'

The truth was that the man who it seemed had just vanished into thin air had in fact been missing for three days. While the *sfincione* was cooking in the oven I had sunk into one of my fantasies and had become so engrossed in the imagined reunion with l'Inglese that first the *sfincione* and then the oven had caught fire before I myself had been overcome by the smoke.

As I lay in my little white bed in the infirmary along-side Nonna Frolla, who had been placed in traction, I wept bitter tears for the beautiful dream that had cheated me, while Nonna Frolla wept inconsolably for the death of the pug.

CHAPTER THREE

I really was very ill. The smoke I had inhaled had badly damaged my lungs and I was left with a racking cough, which tore at my entrails. I remained in the infirmary for several weeks and was fed a diet of thin gruel and a little fruit. The sisters were convinced this was the only food I could digest. As a result I lost a substantial amount of weight, and one day when the nuns were lifting me into my bath I felt thin for the first time in my life.

Nonna Frolla, in traction in the adjoining bed, chattered all day and most of the night. I could have willingly strangled her if I'd had the strength.

The stream of visitors was constant. Nonno Frolla had practically taken up residence at the infirmary and was treated as something of a pet by the sisters on the ward. Each day he brought a rose for Nonna Frolla, but he was still in disgrace over the incident with the widow Palumbo on the night of the fire, and Nonna was determined to make him pay for this for a long time to come.

Despite the whispered explanations of her visitors,

which were accompanied by many gestures and nods towards the adjacent bed where I lay, Nonna Frolla could still not grasp the situation with regard to l'Inglese.

'So where is he?' she would demand of me again and again. 'I don't understand why he doesn't come and visit you.'

My illness gave me an excuse for closing my eyes and feigning sleep.

During the night Nonna would dream of the pug, and would then awaken in the early hours of the morning calling loudly for Nero. She refused to accept that he had died and demanded that Nonno Frolla bring him for a visit. Nonno Frolla went along with the fantasy to avoid hurting his wife with the truth, and began to invent anecdotes about the pug, pretending that it was still alive. It was pathetic to witness Nonna Frolla retelling these stories, suitably embellished, to the visitors who streamed to her bedside. Of course they all knew that the pug was dead and was still lying stiff in the rubbish bin at the corner of the street, but they humoured Nonna Frolla and indulged her in her fantasies.

My dreams were now in black and white and shades of grey. In my weakened state I no longer had the powerful fantasies and daydreams that had led to the fire and its ripple of consequences. My dreams were confined within narrow grey boxes, black and white lines. Faces made mouths at me. White-clad figures hovered in shadows. I had great difficulty in breathing; in my sleep I forgot to breathe.

All I wanted to do was sleep so I could escape from the awful reality of life and exist solely in the grey corridors of my deadened mind. But even sleep evaded me. I could not sleep at night, as that was the only time when I could think, and during the day there was a constant crowd of visitors in the ward and their incessant chatter disturbed me.

All the customers of Nonna Frolla's grocery shop came by at least once a day, as did the tenants of the apartment building. Signor Rivoli, the perverted bank manager, came primarily, I am sure, to try and catch a glimpse of me in a state of undress.

I too received a share of the visitors: all the personnel from the library came. Restituto, the one-eyed replacement doorman, came with gifts of wild strawberries and grapes and books of crossword puzzles that I never opened. He tried to engage my interest by talking about the regular readers, the students, the gossip, but I was not interested, and simply wanted to be left alone, to rest. I found out subsequently that he had completed the circle by marrying Signora Rossi, Crocifisso's widow, and they went on to produce another two *bambini* to add to their cares.

The library assistants led by Costanza came once or twice. She came only to pry, to see if she could enliven the gossip surrounding me back at the library, which had become old news. I stayed resolutely silent when they came and tried to deaden my ears so as not to hear their inane chatter and false laughter. The library girls soon switched their attention to Nonna Frolla, who was able to supply them with all the gossip they needed. They discussed me openly in stage whispers, but even this did not bother me. I lay still and silent and tried to imagine what it was like to be dead. Costanza made a great fuss of Nonno Frolla and once even sat on his lap before the jealous Nonna Frolla administered a sharp slap to her face, which sent the pack of library assistants scurrying from the ward. They did not return.

One day, shortly after my admission to the infirmary, the director of the library came to visit, with his wife, the sophisticated Signora Bandiera. She had a regular weekly appointment at the Per Donna hair parlour and even had the time to apply nail polish. Everyone in the ward looked up at her entrance, which, of course, they were intended to do.

The *signora* had brought in a few of her discarded things for me: a silk scarf that had been damaged by a careless laundrymaid, a string of simulated pearls with a broken clasp, some decorative hairpins, and a bottle of cheap perfume, a gift from a thrifty friend that someone of the *signora*'s sophistication would never wear. I received these gifts graciously, and when the stilted conversation had become embarrassingly slow, the Bandieras got up to leave, satisfied with the feeling that they had done their duty.

I quickly lost track of the passage of time; I knew vaguely in the recesses of my mind that it was autumn, but I did not know which month, date, day, or hour. The days in the infirmary merged into an uninterrupted procession of grey dawns, white sheets, thin gruel, foul-tasting medicines, the unpleasant smell of disinfectant, Nonna Frolla's annoying chatter, and the unending feeling of exhaustion.

I watched the door in a halfhearted way for l'Inglese,

although I knew he would not come. I imagined how it would be if one day he sauntered through the ward in his come-to-bed shoes, his eyes sparkling with mischief, their blue the only colour in my grey world. He would hold me in his arms and everything would be all right; I would come to life again and we would be happy and live and laugh and love and cook as we had that long hot summer not so long ago. And yet in my heart I knew I would never see him again.

One night, some time after the Bandieras' visit, Nonna Frolla failed to wake me with her cries for the pug; she did not snore or chatter in her sleep, and the system of levers and pulleys holding her leg in traction did not creak and strain with her every movement. There was a strange silence hanging heavy on the sterile ether of the ward.

'Nonna, are you all right?' I whispered, my voice sounding curiously loud in the darkness.

There was no reply.

'Nonna . . . ? Nonna . . . ?'

I dragged myself over the side of my bed and rested my feet on the floor; I tested my legs for strength: they held up, just about. Since the night of the fire I had not walked anywhere unaided. I felt like a rag doll walking on its wadding legs.

'Nonna?' I asked again, drawing back the white curtain between our two beds.

Nonna lay peaceful and still and dead. Her little sharp-featured face was still for the first time in 111 years.

Soon the sisters had removed Nonna from the ward, and within minutes no-one would have known that she had ever been there. The sepia photograph of the pug and the vase of flowers were taken away, as were her other few belongings: her reading glasses, her library book, her spare nightgowns and toiletries. The little bed was remade with starched white sheets, and when the other patients woke in the morning no trace of Nonna remained.

When Nonno Frolla came for his early morning visit, bearing the customary rose in his gnarled hand, he found the bed empty. The sisters led him away to the day room to explain that his partner of eighty years had left without him. Then they sent him away with her few things in a brown paper bag.

I insisted on attending the funeral. I was wheeled there in an old bath chair that had been in the attic of the infirmary for decades.

The service took place at the Chiesa di Santa Maria Magdalena, where Nonna was baptized, confirmed, and married all those years ago. Her shrunken form lay in the open casket surrounded by clouds of white organza and rose petals. She was dressed in her little wedding gown of ivory satin. The embalmers had enjoyed complete freedom, taking advantage of Nonno Frolla's age and apparent imbecility, and had endowed Nonna with a Cupid's bow of a fierce scarlet, rouged cheeks, baby blue eyelids, and a head full of kiss curls. The overall impression was obscene.

I wept for the first time when I saw what a travesty death and the mischievous youths of the Serenita Funeral Parlour had made of Nonna. The tears led to a fit of coughing, and the nuns piloting the bath chair saw fit to remove me from the church and propel me back to the infirmary before the proceedings had even begun.

The day after the funeral I lay dozing. It was much quieter now that Nonna had gone; far fewer visitors came to the ward. The regulars from the Frollas' grocery shop stayed away, all except Quinto Cavallo, who continued to bring me thumbed copies of fashion magazines and sometimes pastries. He had grown used to coming to the infirmary, and was unable to give it up. Signor Rivoli, too, continued to come. He now took the liberty of sitting in the vinyl armchair next to my bed, which emitted embarrassing squeaks at every movement. I chose to ignore him, and would often close my eyes when I saw him trotting up the ward and feign sleep through his entire visit. Sometimes he would go away again after an hour or even two without a single word having been exchanged between us. Simply being there was enough for him.

Still, as I lay on my little white bed that afternoon, I heard in my slumbering consciousness a sound I recognized instinctively, a call from the distant past that immediately commanded my attention. Something long ago and far away stirred within me and responded to the call. It was the sound of footsteps, but not regular footsteps. It was the sound of a three-legged gait, a sound unlike any other, a step, a slight drag of a foot, a step and then another step quickly following it. I opened my eyes to see middle-aged male Siamese twins coming towards me along the ward. Although I had not seen them in over twenty-five years, I recognized them immediately as my brothers Guerra and Pace.

Oh my beloved boys! Could it really be them? Despite our long years of separation I had never stopped thinking about them. And here they were, all grown up, and standing right before me at the hospital. I took a long look at them, scarcely believing they were those same little creatures I had looked after as a girl.

They were now well upholstered, and wore a beautifully tailored costume: brown, double-breasted, with a wide pinstripe.

'Boys,' I gasped, overcome with astonishment, 'can it really be you?'

'There are few like us in this world, sister,' was their simultaneous reply.

Tears streamed down my face as we embraced, surrounded by the nuns crossing themselves and fainting, and the other patients on the ward rubbing their eyes in disbelief and imagining themselves to be dreaming. It felt so good to have them hold me in their two strong arms. I made them squeeze me tight to prove I wasn't having one of my daydreams.

'Look at you!' I said again and again, holding them at arm's length and studying them for evidence of those little wily creatures that had been transformed into such strapping full-grown men. I couldn't stop myself crying. It was all too much for one in my weakened state.

We all talked at the same time, we were so excited and so full of questions. We talked for hours, about everything that had happened since that day so long ago when I embarked on my journey to the big city. They had evidently done well for themselves since the old days at Castiglione; they looked comfortable in their matching homburgs, sleek haircuts, and beautiful, hand-crafted shoes. In fact, they were now the wealthiest men in town, and had bought the finest house, which had once been home to the duke. They had set up home with a pock-marked whore called Biancamaria Ossobucco, who serviced the needs of them both simultaneously in an enormous feather bed.

Not a single person or event in the whole history of Castiglione went undiscussed that afternoon in the infirmary. I was more animated that afternoon than I had been since the accident happened. I was almost like my old self. At last, as night began to fall, and the shadows gathered, the twins said simultaneously:

'We've come to take you home, Rosa.'

I did not argue. I realized that the time had come for me to return to Castiglione. The nuns got me dressed in the few things that had been brought in for me by various well-intentioned neighbours; all my belongings had been ruined by the fire. Then the twins helped me outside, where there was a car waiting for us in the street. It was their own, a new model, shipped over specially from the States, with a driver who was to drive us back home. I had never been in a car before: I felt so grand, sinking back into the leather seats while the driver covered me with a travelling rug. The motor purred and we drove along through the darkness. I slipped in and out of sleep; I was warm and comfortable and never wanted the journey to end.

CHAPTER FOUR

It was morning when we reached the *fattoria*. The trees along the Randazzo road were already golden and had begun to lose their leaves; the grapes had long been gathered and the vines were being cut back. The land had given up its bounty of wheat and vegetables and late oranges and bore the look of a plate after a hearty diner had had his fill.

As we approached, I saw a tiny figure making its way towards us along the lane. News travels fast in a small town. I knew while she was still merely a speck in the distance that it was Mama. As we drew closer, sure enough the tiny dot turned into Madre Calabrese. Always tiny even in youth, she had by now shrunk to the size of a pumpkin on legs. Her walk, ever brisk, was rickety. Her hair, previously black streaked with grey, was white.

It was now hard to imagine her as the feisty woman who had ruled the *fattoria* and its community like a dictator. This was the same woman who had shot her second husband, Antonino Calabrese, up the arse with a shotgun, the woman who would not scruple to whip the

212

farmhands if she thought they were slacking off or cheating her.

The car stopped and I climbed out into my mother's arms.

'Rosa, *figlia mia*,' cried Mama, embracing me as tears poured down her wrinkled cheeks.

I too cried; I cried my heart out. I cried all the tears I had not been able to cry in the past months since l'Inglese disappeared, since the accident, since I lost my health, my home, my purpose. The twins too cried and embraced Mother and me. Then from crying we all turned to laughing, wiping away our tears with the backs of our hands, before starting to cry again.

As we stood in the road embracing and crying and laughing, from the pastures, still bearing pitchforks and hoes, came my other brothers, Leonardo, Mario, Giuliano, Giuseppe, Salvatore, and the daft farmhand Rosario. The cycle of crying, laughing, and hugging continued. Isabella Calabrese was not too old to deliver a sharp slap to the cheeks of the daft Rosario when he made so bold a gesture as to embrace me. Not while Mama was alive was one of her farmhands to take liberties with her only daughter.

Helped along by my brothers, I found myself back at the *fattoria*.

The odour of the dark passage made me a child again; the old, slightly musty smell of the house was bound up with being small and having spindly legs and grazed knees that tasted salty when you sucked them. Through all the years it had stayed with me in the remote corners of my memory, and sometimes it had come back to me in

213

my imagination, at night when I was lying awake in my tiny apartment in the Via Vicolo Brugno. But then I could only capture it imperfectly. Now, the smell of cool dark corners, of age-browned plaster, greeted me, remembered me, and told me I was home.

La cucina, at the end of the passage, was unchanged. The past twenty-five years had not made the slightest dent in its appearance. I hoped to find it exactly as I had left it that day when I took the cage of my parrot, Celeste, from the hook by the window and simply walked away. I feared finding anything different. Immediately I registered a few minor changes: the new cushion on the settle, though even that was no longer new; a chair leg that had always been broken was now mended, but reassuringly everything else was the same. It felt as though I had never been away.

I could feel the spirits of my forebears the Fiores all around me. My father was now among them. He sat in his chair smoking a pipe. He was still wearing his beloved mountain cap.

'So you've decided to come back home at last, have you, my girl?' he said between sucks on his pipe.

Nonna Fiore was there too, baking some pies, and Nonno too. You will remember that it was Nonno Fiore whom, according to legend, I had tried to bring back to life with a dish of *panelle* when I was about four. Other shadows were there too; ghosts had always lived in the *cucina* of the Fiores.

I wandered around the kitchen, touching the lustre of the table, the gleaming pans lined up along the wall, assuring myself that my homecoming was real.

Everything was just as it had always been, even the tea that Mama handed me, made with the iron-coloured well water and tasting like no other tea on earth.

Soon breakfast was ready and I sat down with my brothers and the rest of the farmhands. The heavenly aroma of Mama's homemade bread fresh from the oven made me feel hunger for the first time in weeks.

When Mama was satisfied there were no dirty hands at her table, she ladled out steaming bowls of thick bean soup, and heaped the table with prosciutto, eggs, goat's cheese, olives, and strong black coffee.

After breakfast the twins left to attend to their business affairs, and the farm workers went back to the fields, leaving my mother and me alone in the kitchen. I went out in the yard with the scraps and leftovers and scraped them into the trough for the dogs. It was a beautiful morning, crisp and clear and still. The dogs were the descendants of the dogs that I had known and fussed over and fed in the past. They hung back from this stranger giving them their breakfast and only came forward to eat when I had gone back inside.

Then, over a fresh pot of brackish tea, Mama and I sat down to talk about everything that had happened since our separation.

'And so Mother, what exactly happened with Antonino Calabrese?' I asked, tracing patterns on the glossy wooden surface of the table as I had always done since I was tiny.

Mama paused before answering.

'It happened so long ago now, daughter, that I hardly even remember it. Let me see now. Well, of course he wasn't from farming stock. The ways of the farm didn't suit him. He didn't like the work, and I wouldn't keep a man who didn't work his way. Anyway things gradually soured between us. We started to argue more and more, and he started to stay out late at nights in the tavern in the town; he took to drinking hard, and the more he drank, the more we quarrelled, and so on. It must be twenty years ago now, when the final straw came.

'One Tuesday it was, I remember it quite well now, although I thought I couldn't remember any of it. In the afternoon I went into the dairy to check on the butter; three pans of butter there were, and two of cheese. That strumpet of a dairymaid Balbina Burgondofara was nowhere to be seen. She left my butter and cheeses unattended, and disappeared somewhere, probably for a quick embrace with one of the farmhands. I'll have her, I thought to myself, leaving my butters to turn rancid and my cheeses to curdle. I'll give her a sound whipping, I thought, and her beau too. Quietly I crept into the cowshed, the one where you had stored all those barrels of ricotta, and sure enough, beyond the stalls, in the mound of fresh straw at the far end, I came upon our young lovers. He with his pink arse stuck up in the air was not one of the farmhands. No. The pink arse belonged to my own husband, Antonino Calabrese.

'I murmured not a word, despite my fury. Resisting the very strong temptation to launch an attack on them there and then, I let not a single sound betray my presence. I crept, quietly as an angel, out of the cowshed and back into the house to get Father's shotgun. I always kept it fully loaded at the side of the bed, just in case I should ever need it to fend off the bandits. I also supplied myself with a good strong whip from the tack room.

'Once again I tiptoed into the cowshed, this time armed and ready. Our lovers were still going at it hammer and tongs. With one lunge I thrust the barrel of the shotgun between Antonino Calabrese's buttocks and pulled the trigger. It took that stupid girl Balbina Burgondofara some time to catch on, so transported was she by the prowess of my husband. The look of horror on her face when she finally realized was wonderful to see. I whipped her within an inch of her life, and then some more for her impudence.

'Your brothers took the corpse and buried it among the trees in the upper pasture. We didn't want the *carabinieri* nosing around. We just let it be known around the town that he had gone back to the mainland, and no-one ever asked any questions. So that was the end of that. Since then, of course, I've had other friends, but I like to have the bed to myself now that I'm older.'

Mama's black eyes were fiery again with the recollection of her story.

'Tell me, Rosa,' she said, pouring another cup of tea. 'What happened with that Inglese, the one that Luigi sent me the telegram about?'

'I'm glad you mentioned that, Mama. What I want to know is: how did Luigi know about him?'

'He never said.'

'Well, what did he say?'

'Only what I wrote to you. Wait, I've got the telegram here somewhere.'

I held my breath as she scrabbled about in Nonna

Calzino's enormous silver teapot, where she kept her odds and ends. Perhaps the telegram would provide the answers to all my questions. I was about to burst with impatience as she pored over torn scraps of photographs, keys to unknown locks, and decayed memorabilia and the associated stories I could see she was struggling to remember. There didn't appear to be a telegram in the pile she had tipped out onto the table.

'Mama, the telegram?' I reminded her. She was certainly more forgetful now than she had been.

'Oh, the telegram,' she said absentmindedly, surfacing from the shadowy world of her memories. 'It's not here. I must have used it for lighting the fire.'

I wanted to scream. The telegram could have provided a clue to the mystery that was constantly turning over in my mind. What did Luigi know about l'Inglese? How did he know? Was there some connection between them? Was Luigi involved in l'Inglese's disappearance? Did Luigi know what had happened to him?

'Wait!' said Mama, seeing the despair in my face. 'I can remember what was in the telegram. Wait a minute. Let me think.' She closed her eyes, summoning up the power of her fading memory.

'I remember it now,' she said triumphantly after a pause. 'It said: "Mama. Palermo says Rosa acting the *puttana* with Inglese. Dishonouring the family. Stop her. I send you $500. Lui." '

'Was that all he said? Are you sure that was all?'

'I may be old now,' said Mama, narrowing her black eyes at me, 'but my yarn is not yet unravelled. That is all he said.'

This was no more than I knew already. It didn't give me anything new to go on. Perhaps I was reading too much into Luigi's telegram. Perhaps he had just heard some gossip about his sister. Maybe there was no connection with l'Inglese. Maybe I had got it wrong. I didn't know what to think any more. All those weeks in the hospital it had been running endlessly through my mind. I was so tired of thinking.

'So what happened to him? The Inglese?' asked Mama.

'He disappeared. Just like Papa. I went to his house to meet him and he had gone, leaving all his things behind. I searched and searched but there was no trace of him anywhere. I just knew he had gone for good.'

'It's probably for the best, you know, Rosa. Luigi didn't like it. He didn't like it at all.'

'It had nothing to do with Luigi, Mama. Absolutely nothing. I'm not a child any more, and I'll do as I like.' I started coughing in my anger. I coughed so much I couldn't talk for a long while and had to drink several cups of water. The pain had returned to my lungs.

'It's all right, Rosa, don't get yourself upset. It doesn't matter now.'

'I'm not upset.'

'Yes, you are. You've gone purple. Even as a child you went purple when you were upset.'

'Mama, please don't be argumentative.'

'All right, Rosa, calm yourself, do. Now tell me something else, how did the fire start in your apartment building? I've heard it was arson.'

'No, it wasn't arson. I was daydreaming . . .'

'I might have known . . .' Mama interrupted, rolling her eyes upward.

'I had left a fine *sfincione* in the oven and didn't notice when it started to burn. I knew nothing about it until the firemen broke in and carried me outside, choking. I was taken by ambulance to the infirmary. I stayed a long time until Guerra and Pace came for me.'

'I know, Rosa. Luigi sent us a telegram from Chicago saying you had been involved in an accident. He told the twins to come and bring you home.'

'How did Luigi know?' It was spooky the way he seemed to know everything about me.

'He makes it his business to know everything. They say he has his spies everywhere. Nothing happens on the whole of the island but that he knows about it. It saves me the trouble of writing to him, Rosa, for he knows all my business almost before I know it myself. I never did like writing letters.'

'Well, I'm pleased he sent the twins, anyway. It was so good to see them at the hospital, walking into the ward in their smart suits, looking like a pair of businessmen. They seem to be doing very well for themselves.'

'Hmmm,' Mama replied with a strong look of disapproval, colouring her face grey. 'They look well enough, and they have lots of money, it's true; but I worry about them, Rosa. They're mixed up in all sorts of things, shady things, dark dealings. They'll come to a bad end, Rosa; I can feel it in my blood. And they live with a whore, did they tell you that? The three of them sleeping together in a big bed they had imported especially. By the grace of the blessed Virgin. Three in a bed.'

'Well, they could hardly sleep apart, Mother, could they now?'

Mama's face twisted in disdain.

'I don't like it, Rosa, it brings disgrace on the family, sons of the Fiores setting up home with a pockmarked whore. Biancamaria Ossobuco: there's not a man in the region that hasn't had it with that one. Her rates are lower than anyone else's, bargain prices. She just wouldn't get any custom otherwise. And there are my sons setting her up in their home just as if she was a fine lady. It's a disgrace. An absolute disgrace. I won't have her in the house. I've told them that. I won't let her in. So they need not even try bringing her round here. I'll not have her and that's that.'

'Now, Mother, I think you're being unfair. If they're happy with her then that should be good enough for us. The poor boys can't pick and choose. Let us not forget that.'

'That's what Luigi says, but I can't like it, Rosa, I just can't.'

CHAPTER FIVE

The following week I was feeling so much stronger that I made a trip into town. As I set foot in the piazza, a throng of schoolchildren in pinafores started dancing around me.

'Rosa Fiore is home. It's Rosa Fiore. Rosa Fiore. Rosa Fiore,' they trilled in squeaky voices.

I was surprised to find that a new generation of local children knew who I was, even though I had left town when their parents were children themselves. But this was not in itself so amazing. My story had become folklore and was still told by grandmothers on a winter's evening before a roaring fire. In some versions I had run away to join a travelling circus on the mainland; in another I had become a pirate like my forefather Pasquale Fiore and in yet another I had travelled as far as Paris to become a famous showgirl of somewhat shadowy repute. None of the stories told of how I took the autobus to Palermo and worked as a librarian. Nevertheless the children delighted to see the subject of a legend walking and living and breathing among them.

As I crossed the piazza I saw Padre Francesco going

into the *chiesa*. He was bent over now with age and his hair was white. I had never been to confession since that very day when the priest had masturbated over the account of my initiation into the mysterious rites of sex while my young lover was already lying dead with his throat cut by his father's hand.

I walked slowly up the hill to the cemetery; my lungs still hurt at the least exertion and I had to keep stopping and resting. I swung the gate open and had a sudden flash of memory. I saw myself lying on the ground out-side this very gate all those years ago on the day of the funeral when they would not let me inside. My lungs were hurting then too: from the sobs that tore at them.

I walked past the rows of white stones bearing their inscriptions and sepia photographs of the dead. They all looked back at me, fresh-faced and smiling. Did people have these studio portraits taken with this in mind?

I walked straight to Bartolomeo's grave. It was care-fully tended: the stone was polished, there was no trace of dust. There were no weeds poking through the surround-ing gravel, and while most of the other graves had artificial flowers of violent blues and reds, on his were fresh blooms, thoughtfully arranged and obviously laid out this morning. I wondered who took such care of it. I would have liked to say thank you.

I knelt down before the grave where my Bartolomeo lay. I could scarcely believe so much time had passed since his death. Coming back here made it all feel recent again. I felt the incisions in the stone, recording his name and the dates of his birth and his death. The chiselled edges were not so sharp now, having been washed by the rain of twenty-five winters. Winters that I had lived through without him.

I started telling Bartolomeo all the things that had happened since I went away. I started at the beginning and told him everything. I told him about my bus journey to Palermo. About my job in the library. My lodgings in the Via Vicolo Brugno. Nonna Frolla and her grocery shop. The director, Crocifisso, Costanza, and Signor Rivoli.

Then I told him about l'Inglese. I was sure he would not mind that I had managed to find love with another. It had nothing to do with the love that I still felt for him, and always would. I felt a little shy at first, admitting these things to him, but as I talked on my confidence grew and I told him all. I told him how l'Inglese had first come to the library, and how I was so attracted to him but tried to fight it. And then, when I stopped fighting it, how wonderful it was, and how I felt alive, and, for the first time, like a woman. I told him about our lovemaking, and our cooking. I told him how funny and wild and passionate l'Inglese was. How he made me do crazy things that I'd never done before. And how I loved him. And how now he too was gone. And I was alone again. And trying to hold myself together the best I could.

And then I stopped talking and had a little cry. And then I thought I shouldn't let Bartolomeo see me upset, because that would upset him, so I stopped crying and told him about the fire in my apartment, and my spell in the infirmary, and how the twins had come to bring me home. I told him how Mama had shot Antonino Calabrese, how the twins had found happiness with

Biancamaria Ossobuco, and how Luigi had become a pizza millionaire in Chicago.

It was late when I finally finished talking. I had been kneeling at the grave for hours and my legs and back had gone stiff. I kissed Bartolomeo's youthful photograph and limped away.

As I made my way back to the *fattoria* I felt glad I had confided in Bartolomeo. I was pleased at the symmetry: I had told l'Inglese about Bartolomeo, and now I had told Bartolomeo about l'Inglese. I felt it was right there should be a bridge between the two loves of my life.

Once I arrived back at the farm, my legs walked me into *la cucina*, and instinctively I rolled up my sleeves and tied on my apron. It was time for me to make myself at home once more in the kitchen. The glossy aubergines nestling in a basket invited me to make a *caponata*, a sweet-and-sour vegetable stew.

I sliced and salted the aubergines and left them to disgorge their bitter juices. While waiting, I chopped an onion and some tomatoes and celery on the old table. The blade of the knife became a blur in my fast-moving fingers. I chopped for Bartolomeo, a beautiful young life so needlessly cut down. I chopped for l'Inglese, who I knew in my heart was also dead: no-one ever survived a disappearance. And I chopped for myself, for the happiness that was always snatched away from me. The vegetables soon became very small dice.

When I had wiped the aubergines I fried them in some of Mama's best olive oil, then set them to drain while I fried the onion, and added the tomatoes and a good pinch of salt. When the sauce had thickened I put in a handful

225

of capers, the celery, and two handfuls of green olives, and left the dish to simmer for a while. This caused a delicious perfume to emerge from the open door of *la cucina*, and led old Rosario, loitering in the yard, to say, 'Ahh, Rosa's home.' Rosario had been loitering in the yard my whole life. When the time came we would have to bury him there.

Then I added the fried aubergines, a little sugar, and a little wine vinegar, and cooked it just long enough for the vinegar to evaporate.

I waited impatiently for the *caponata* to cool a little, and then ate it up with some chunks of fresh bread. It felt good to be home.

CHAPTER SIX

The mild golden days of autumn grew shorter and cooler. They became grey; the sun grew weaker, its rays no longer warmed the earth. I had by now grown used to being back at Castiglione; my years in the city seemed a long-closed chapter now. I did not hunger for city ways: my life was here again.

I was growing stronger in the clean country air, on a diet of wholesome home produce. I had begun to regain the weight I had lost after the accident; colour had returned to my cheeks; I looked somehow younger now; in fact one or two of the men in the village were said to be interested in courting me, but I dismissed such notions as ridiculous. I would never love again. What man could match l'Inglese? There was not another like him. And now that my eyes had been opened, how could I settle for a lesser man? I couldn't.

Still I dreamed of l'Inglese. I looked forward to the nights, when I could retreat from the bustle of the farming day into my old room, and embracing sleep I hoped for dreams. But even in my dreams l'Inglese was elusive. I would find him at last after wading through quicksand, crossing deserts, navigating rough seas, walking for miles in the heat of the sun, but whenever I arrived at my journey's end, and with indescribable joy found him, and reached out for him, and saw his own two arms reaching out for me, I would always, at the very point of touching him, wake up. Afterwards, crushed with disappointment, I would will myself to return to the dream, to recapture the happy ending I had been cheated of. How I longed to touch him, to feel him, to kiss him, to hold him, to feel the heart-bursting elation of our reunion, but when the spell of the dream was broken, my imagination was unable to rise to the challenge, and I was left feeling empty, cold, and alone.

Such were my exhausting nights. My days were less arduous. There was no quicksand for me to traverse. No high seas. Just mountains of pasta and lakes of soup to be prepared for the hungry farmhands.

Winter drew on, with its crisp cold mornings and evenings spent in *la cucina* in front of the burning fire, with all of us telling stories and gossiping. Invariably the ghost of Nonna Fiore would appear at these times and regale those gathered with her comic and often obscene tales of life at the *fattoria* in the last century. Sometimes we had to send her away, she was so disgraceful, especially if we had company.

The days leading up to Christmas were filled with a flurry of activity in preparation for the feast days. For me, it was almost like the days of my youth, so taken up was I with the plucking of pheasants and the making of pies, marzipan, cakes, and all manner of Christmas fare.

Mama had decided which of her pigs was due for slaughter, and felt it was only right that I should be given the honour of butchering it. I sharpened my knives on the steel, back and forth, back and forth a thousand times; there came the smooth sound of metal on metal, and the smell of warmed steel and the sweat from my exertions.

I bound up my hair, to keep it free of the blood that would be carefully gathered and made into sausages, and rolled my sleeves above the elbows. Then, putting on a pair of rubber boots and a coarse apron, I took my knives, my saw, my sterilized basins, and my buckets of boiling water out into the yard to the pen where the poor porker had been segregated from its family and stood waiting for me.

The pig looked up at me in sorrow; it saw its death in my eyes and grunted piteously. It had been over twenty-five years since I had slaughtered an animal, but I did not feel squeamish. I took its head in my arms and stuck it with my sharpest knife in the throat, just in front of the breastbone. Feeling the bone against the knife I let the knife slip forward to go under it, and then pushed it in a couple of inches more, slicing with the point of the knife towards the head. As I severed the artery the porker seemed to come to life again and thrashed around, kicking with its hooves. As the blood gushed forth from the gaping wound in the neck I was quick to position my buckets underneath to gather it up for my sausages, deftly replacing one with another once it became full.

Then, hauling my pig onto its side, I began the scraping. To do this you need to pour hot water over a small area and then, once the bristles have become loosened, you scrape at them furiously with a special scraping knife. The secret is to keep working until the pig is absolutely clean.

I submerged each of the trotters in a bucket of hot water, and soaked them slightly. I was then able to pull off the horny toes with a hook. Then I doused the pig with cold water to remove all the loose skin, bristles, and traces of blood.

Next, I sawed through the breastbone and hung the pig up by the tendons in its hind legs. Cutting carefully between the hams, I hauled out the guts, which flopped down into a basin waiting below. Finally I threw several buckets of cold water inside and outside the carcass to clean it thoroughly, then, propping it open with some sticks, I left it to stiffen overnight. Throwing the lungs to the sheepdogs as a special treat, I gathered up the buckets of blood for the sausages, and the intestines and other entrails that needed to be washed.

When all was done I came in from the yard, my face and forearms smeared with blood; straggly bits of hair had escaped from the bunch I had tied it in and got in my eyes. In *la cucina* I found Mama slumped in a heap over the table.

'Mama!' I screamed, dropping the knife and the pail of blood I was carrying. It went all over the floor, soaking my feet and the hem of my dress and the flagstones.

'Mama!'

I rushed over and lifted Mama's head up from the pillow of dough where it had come to rest. Mama let out a low-pitched groan that showed she was still just alive.

'Mama, Mama, speak to me. Don't die, please don't die,' I cried, choking back tears.

Mama groaned again and seemed to be trying to say something.

'What is it, Mama?' I asked. 'What is it you want to say? Shall I call the priest?'

A flicker of Mama's eyes showed this was not what she wanted.

'Rosa,' she murmured finally in a rasping voice that showed the extent of her suffering.

'My girl,' she said very slowly, gasping for breath, 'there is something I have to tell you.' Here she lurched with a sudden spasm of pain.

'You don't have to say anything, Mama; don't try and talk, just rest and I'll run and fetch the doctor.'

'No, Rosa, it's too late for the doctor. Listen to me, there's something I have to tell you before I die.'

'Mama, you won't die, please let me get help, allow me to call the doctor.'

'No, Rosa. Listen to me. I haven't much time left. I need to tell you something very important.' She swallowed hard.

'Rosa, your father was not your father.'

'What?'

'I mean, the man you knew as your father, Filippo Fiore, was not really your father.'

My mouth had fallen wide with shock.

'No, my girl, anyone with half an eye could see you were not his child. Your true father was . . .' Here Mama's breath grew thicker and more laboured.

'He was . . .'

Her breath was now so heavy it seemed to be the only sound in the world. The death rattle was in her throat. Making one final stupendous effort, her tiny frame shaking, she said:

'Rosa, your father was . . .'

But she could not finish the sentence before her neck went limp and her head fell forward again into the dough ball that had risen to massive proportions on the ancient table.

'Mama, Mama, Mama! No! Oh no! No!' I screamed, cradling Mama's lifeless body in my arms and rocking her back and forth, willing her to wake up again.

'No, no, no,' I sobbed, willing that it was not so. Willing that there had been some mistake; willing that her time had not yet come. I stayed like that, rocking my mother in my arms, for a long time. I could not let her go. And while I rocked I cried and cried the most bitter tears, which ran down my cheeks and plopped onto Mama's.

Mama had only just come back into my life, and I was only just reaching an understanding with her that we had never had when I was younger; and now here she was gone. Another death. Another loss. How much mourning should one woman have to do in a lifetime? I felt that I had already done too much.

I may have imagined it, but I clearly remember the ghost of Nonna Calzino appearing to me then as I cradled Mama in the gathering darkness.

'You have to let her go, Rosa,' she said simply. 'It's her time.'

I was still sobbing and rocking Mama when the boys,

Leonardo, Mario, Giuliano, Giuseppe, and Salvatore, returned to the *fattoria* from the fields for supper.

On seeing the scene of carnage in the kitchen – the discarded knife with the blood-soaked blade and the huge pool of blood darkening the flagstones – and then coming upon the figure of their sister, in a state of disarray, bending over their mother's body, their one immediate thought was that there had been the most dreadful accident.

'Rosa, what have you done?' asked Leonardo with a look of horror in his eyes as he regarded me in the light of a murderess, worse still, a matricide.

'Mama is dead,' I bawled, my tears flowing anew as I was forced to confront the reality of the situation by explaining it to the others. 'I came in from slaughtering the pig and found her hunched over the table; she only lasted a few moments. I didn't have time to fetch you or call the doctor; as I was holding her she just slipped away.'

My brothers looked at each other, each thinking the same thought: that I had gone mad and killed our mother. Leonardo signalled to Mario, Giuliano, Giuseppe, and Salvatore, indicating that they should follow him outside.

'Mario, you run into town with Giuliano and fetch the doctor. Salvatore, you go with them and get the police: tell them that Rosa has murdered Mama. Giuseppe, you round up a few of the lads in case things turn nasty. I'll try and keep her calm until you get back, now hurry.'

Mario, Giuliano, Salvatore, and Giuseppe ran off as fast as they could and Leonardo came back into the kitchen to deal with his crazy sister.

'Rosa, why don't you put Mama down?' he asked me in the tone of voice we all used on the simpleton Rosario.

'I just want to hold her a little longer, Leo. I don't want her to get cold.'

'Come on now, Rosa, put her down. We need to lay her out flat on the table, otherwise she'll set in that position and grow hard and we won't be able to get her in the coffin. You don't want that, do you now?'

I reluctantly relinquished my grip and helped Leonardo place the tiny body on the table. Unfortunately the corpse was covered in blood that must have come from its contact with me, bloodied as I was from the slaughter; my handprints in blood were on Mama's cheeks and hands and clothes.

Leonardo picked up the knife when he saw my head was turned and kept it clenched in his grasp behind his back in case, as he said afterwards, the situation worsened. Presumably he thought I was going to attack him. After what seemed like ages his reinforcements arrived. His relief was palpable.

The old family doctor, Dr Leobino, entered while the two officers of the *carabinieri* flanked the door in case I tried to escape. They both had their pistols cocked and ready. In the background, at a safe distance, hovered the despicable Padre Francesco.

'Now, Rosa,' said Dr Leobino, gingerly approaching the table where Mama was lying and where I was standing with my arms folded across my chest, 'tell me what has happened here.'

'Doctor. Mama is dead.'

'Can I take a look at her?'

234

'Yes, Doctor, but I don't think anything can be done.'

'Well, let me just have a little look.'

He carefully examined the body for wounds, but of course, could not find any.

'You're quite right, Rosa, nothing can be done for her now. Tell me, how did she die?'

'I had been slaughtering the pig for Christmas night, Doctor. As I came inside from the yard I saw Mama slumped over the table; she was kneading dough, and her head had fallen into it. I knew something was wrong. In my panic I dropped the bucket containing the blood with which I was going to make my special sausages . . .'

'Ah yes, I've never tasted a sausage to rival one of yours, Rosa,' interrupted the doctor.

'And the blood spilled all over the floor. I ran over to Mama. I thought she was dead, but she was still just alive. I pulled her up out of the dough. She tried to say something to me but she couldn't breathe. I told her to wait while I called you and the boys, but she said there wasn't time. She sort of gasped and choked and made a funny sound in her throat and then her head dropped down and I knew that she was dead. I held her for a long time in my arms; I didn't want to let her go. Did I do wrong, Doctor?'

'No, Rosa, you haven't done anything wrong. I am most sorry for you in your grief. Your mother was a good woman. May she rest in peace with the Lord.'

Then, turning to the officers of the *carabinieri*, he said, 'Come, gentlemen, I don't think we are needed here,' and with that he swept out of *la cucina*, past my brothers, who were all looking rather sheepish.

235

' "Sister has murdered Mother" indeed,' muttered the doctor under his breath as he passed Giovanni in the passage.

Assured that all was safe and that I was not about to run him through with my filleting knife, Padre Francesco entered from the yard. He performed the rites and in the process himself became smeared with blood. The blood on the floor soaked into the hem of his crisp white chasuble as it brushed the flagstones, and when he left he looked as though he had been administering the last rites in a war zone.

We laughed about it afterwards, but I have never forgotten that my brothers thought me capable of matricide.

CHAPTER SEVEN

The funeral was delayed for a few days to allow Luigi time to take an aeroplane over from Chicago. An aeroplane! No-one had ever heard of anyone who had flown in an aeroplane.

The wait was extremely inconvenient because Mama was laid out on the kitchen table. Meals had to be taken with my brothers and the farmhands and myself crowded around one end of the table, while Mama presided at the other.

I had done my best with my mother's corpse. I had dressed her in one of her best nightgowns and had woven some artificial flowers into her hair. Around her I had placed jars of scented leaves and berries; there were not many flowers around at this time of year, and I knew Mama would disapprove of any unnecessary expense at a florist's. Candles were kept lit day and night. Fortunately the weather was cold and the liberal dousings of eau de cologne I sprinkled all over the corpse were sufficient to stop it from reeking.

Christmas was a miserable time, although we all

237

pretended to enjoy ourselves. The roast pork was succulent with my special crackling, as crunchy and crisp as any that could be imagined. I served it with a sauce of home-grown apples, some roast potatoes with rosemary, and some mountain spinach. The porker was tender, there was no debate on that; she had been well slaughtered, all had to agree. It was acknowledged by all that I was an expert with a filleting knife.

At last, on New Year's Eve, Luigi arrived from the States with his wife, the barmaid from Linguaglossa. They looked like film stars. The barmaid even had a fur coat that she twirled in my face the second she stepped inside. She was too grand for the old place now and wrinkled her nose at the dust and the cobwebs and my housekeeping; she herself had a maid in Chicago.

She screamed on seeing the corpse, saying how grotesque it was and how pleased she was she had not brought the children: such a thing would surely give them nightmares for life. She had brought so much baggage with her that the weight of it nearly induced a hernia in the daft farmhand Rosario, whose lot was to carry it inside, and he was accustomed to heavy work on the farm. She seemed to regard the whole trip as nothing more than a fashion parade, and throughout the visit she changed her clothes at least four times a day.

Luigi was lenient with her. He had more important things on his mind. He had grown fat on his diet of pizza in Chicago and he went everywhere with the end of a cigar clamped between his teeth. From the time he arrived to the time he left, a stream of shiny cars came up the lane to the house, a succession of strange men in suits got out of them, and Luigi spent hours closeted away in meetings with these strangers, so it was virtually impossible for the rest of us to speak to him.

The funeral could be delayed no longer, and took place on the morning of New Year's Day. It was unusually cold as our little procession made its way up the hillside to the Chiesa di Ave Maria, and on to the cemetery. This was the third time I had made this journey; my lover, the empty coffin of the man I now feared wasn't my father, and now, finally, my mother I had followed up this hill. Soon it would be my own turn.

We passed the grave of Bartolomeo; he smiled at me, still a boy, from the photograph set in the stone. How strange that he should stay young and I should grow old and stout; what an odd couple we would make now, I thought.

The procession stopped at the Fiore plot. The ground next to Papa's empty tomb had been opened up to receive Mama.

Padre Francesco officiated; he made a living out of burying my loved ones.

'*In nomine padre, filii, et spiritu sanctus . . .*'

Luigi had arranged for a group of professional singers to be brought all the way from Agrigento, and as they sang the Ave Maria, the tiny coffin was lowered into the ground.

As we walked home, the mourners fell into groups of ones and twos chatting about the things one invariably talks about after funerals. I found myself walking along with Luigi. Fortunately we were out of earshot of the others, although the strident voice of the barmaid from

Linguaglossa could be heard resounding from some way away. There was something I had to ask him. Of all my brothers, Luigi would know the truth.

'Luigi, Mama talked a little to me before she died.'

'She did?' He spoke now with an American accent.

'Yes.'

'Well, what did she say?'

'It was difficult to make out as her breathing was so irregular and she really was on the brink of death, but I'm sure she said that Papa was not my real father.'

'Oh, so she told you that.'

'Do you mean it's true?'

'Yeah, it's true.'

I felt as though I had been hit in the stomach with a fist, just below the rib cage. I could hardly breathe. So it was true. Naively I was hoping he was going to say that Mama's mind was wandering as death came closer and that she had somehow invented it all.

'I know it must have come as a shock to you, Rosa, hearing it in that way, too, but it's true, you were not born from Filippo Fiore's seed.'

'So who is my real father, do you know, Lui?'

'I did hear some things, of course, but Rosa, Papa always looked on you as his little girl. You know I think he believed you were his. I don't think he ever knew, ever suspected, even. Certainly you were always his favourite. It didn't make no difference to him. It was all such a long time ago now, are you sure you really want to know?'

'Of course I do. I need to know. There's no going back now. Tell me who it is.'

'It happened like this. Mama, when she was younger, was a very passionate woman. She always enjoyed the company of men. It wasn't that she didn't love Papa or anything like that. When she was young, if a man showed an interest in her, it was very difficult for her to refuse him. It didn't mean nothing to her. Nothing at all. It was just a physical thing.'

'So who was it, Luigi? Don't keep me in suspense.'

'All right, I'm coming to that. I'm just explaining a bit of the background to you first.'

'Lui,' I pleaded.

'All right, have it your own way. It was the priest.'

'Padre Francesco?'

'Yeah.'

'You're telling me that the priest, Padre Francesco, is my father?'

'Yeah. I'm sorry to break it to you like that, but you forced it out of me. It don't make no difference to the rest of us. You're still our little sister.'

Padre Francesco, the pervert priest. I could not believe it. My flesh crawled. Luigi dropped behind, sensing that I needed to be alone to digest this most unwelcome piece of news. Oh, that it were not so. That there had been some mistake. The priest was abhorrent to me. All my life I had felt a repugnance for him, especially at the time of Bartolomeo's death, when he had abused my trust, denied me the protection of the church, and masturbated at my story. I had never spoken a single word to him again, and from then on I had turned my back on the church that he represented. To think that I was the issue of such a man was just too horrible to bear. While the man that I had always thought of as my father, the kind, simple, decent Filippo Fiore, was no more than a cuckold. Perhaps he had hated me, the visible evidence of his wife's infidelity.

After asking about my father, I had intended to go on and ask Lui what he knew about l'Inglese, but this news was such a shock I couldn't take any more just then. As I marched along towards the *fattoria* I heard the distinctive sound of the twins clattering along the path behind me. I turned and they limped alongside with their strange three-legged gait. They were smiling shyly.

'Rosa, we have something to tell you. There is some joy to be had on this sad day after all. Rosa, we wanted you to be the first to know; we are going to be a father.'

'Oh boys, that's lovely. I'm very happy for you both. For all of you.' I tried to sound enthusiastic, but it was difficult given that I just wanted to start screaming and never stop.

'Thank you. We only found out this very morning. Biancamaria Ossobuco is with child. Our child. It does not matter to us which of us is the father. There is no way of knowing, and besides, we are one flesh. It will be our child. The doctor says it has every chance of being born normal, and if it's a girl, we will name her after you.'

'I would be honoured. I am so pleased for you, I really am. We need some good news, boys, for there is too much misery in this world.'

They scampered away with a spring in their joint step to tell their brothers of their joy. How Mama would have hooted. The whore to bear a child. Suppose it too was born with the curse of deformity like its fathers? My head was heavy with the weight of these thoughts.

Soon we were home and I prepared the tea, which I served in the front parlour. There was prosciutto in abundance from the slaughtered porker, and bread and pickles. None of us could quite fancy it; it was too painful a reminder of the awful day of Mama's death; but the barmaid from Linguaglossa ate enough to make herself sick, and the distant relatives and the villagers observed few niceties. There was cold pheasant too and some apple tart with quince to follow. Mama would have been pleased with the spread. As soon as they had all gone, I tidied away the dishes and took myself up to bed. I had too much to think over. It had been a horrible day.

The following day Luigi and the barmaid from Linguaglossa were to return to the States. Just as they were climbing into the car to go to the airport, I knew it was now or never: I had to ask Luigi what he knew about l'Inglese.

'That man was no good, Rosa. I didn't like it when I heard you had started fooling around with him. A no-good piece of trash, that's all he was. That's why I had him removed.'

The driver started the engine.

'Removed?' I asked, not following him.

The car began to pull away. I walked alongside, by the open window. Everyone started waving them goodbye.

'I had him taken out,' I heard Luigi say above the shouts of goodbye and the noise of the engine. 'You won't be seeing him again.'

I could no longer keep pace with the vehicle.

'You mean he's dead? You had him killed?' I shouted after him. But it was too late, Luigi had gone. I was never to see him again. The next year he was found in an underground car park with a bullet through his brain. But again I am getting ahead of myself.

I hurried to *la cucina* and began pounding at some dough for the evening bread. So my brother had killed my lover. What a way to start the day.

I pounded and pounded at the dough with such force that the venerable table shook on its legs. Now my mother was dead, the priest was my father, and my brother had killed my lover. For the first time in my life I feared for my sanity. Suddenly I could feel everything slipping through my grasp. My fists came down on the dough with a crash. Just what else were the fates going to throw at me?

So my supposition had been correct: Luigi's henchmen were not interested in me at all, but in l'Inglese. But how? Why?

How did Luigi know him? It could only mean that l'Inglese was somehow mixed up in Mafia affairs: after all, that was Luigi's world. How could the two of them be connected?

Why had Luigi said l'Inglese was no good? What did he know of him to make him think that?

I had often found myself mulling over l'Inglese's words: that he could not tell me where he had been on that trip out of Palermo at the time of Crocifisso's death, or what he had been doing, 'for my own safety.' When the danger was past, he said, he would tell me everything. Clearly this had little to do with writing cookery books.

How I wished I had pressed him further at the time, and made him tell me. But I was so in love with him I had just accepted everything.

Now I would never know; my brother had had l'Inglese killed. I knew I would get nothing further out of Luigi, even if somehow I managed to pursue him on the other side of the globe. I knew also that even if I drove myself completely mad considering all the possibilities, it would still not bring l'Inglese back.

L'Inglese was dead. I had felt it, that he was dead, before now. In my heart I had known it all along. Objectively I knew no one survived a disappearance. Yet up until this time, when I knew it for sure, I had always liked to fool myself with the hope that by some miracle, in the future, however distant, we might come together again. Now all hope was gone. He was dead. That so alive, so vital man was dead. I tried to imagine it, but couldn't. I forced myself to imagine his corpse, to make myself believe it. How could that life force so strong in him be extinguished like the insignificant flame of a candle? I couldn't accept it. I hated Luigi. I punched at the dough as though punching him in the face. I had not kneaded like this since Bartolomeo's death.

CHAPTER EIGHT

The following day I went into town, as I had business
with my father the priest. My mental turmoil gave speed
to my legs, and I was almost running by the time I
reached the *chiesa*.

I entered to find Padre Francesco tending the altar,
much as I had done that day twenty-six years ago
after my night of love with Bartolomeo. The perfume of
incense, the flickering candles, and the weeping statue
of Our Lady brought that day back to me with a horrible
clarity.

Now the *padre* was bent over with age and his
hair, once as black as peat, was white and sparse. His
face was lined with furrows and his eyesight had
dimmed.

'Hello, Father,' I called out with unconscious irony.

'Who's there?' he jumped, hearing a strange voice
behind him.

'It is Rosa.'

'Rosa?' he said, his voice forming a question mark.

'Rosa . . .' musing to himself.

He shuffled closer and fixed me with eyes glazed with cataracts. Recognition dawned slowly.

'Ah, my child. I know you. I know your face, although I cannot remember your name . . .'

'My name is Rosa Fiore,' I said quietly.

Was I imagining it, or did his composure falter for a second?

'Ah yes, Rosa. Rosa Fiore.' He repeated the sounds softly to himself as if to aid his memory. 'I knew your parents.'

'You knew my mother quite well, didn't you, Padre?'

'Yes, I did. Why do you ask?'

'Because there are some things I need to know. Some things I want to ask you.'

'I see. Well then, come into the vestry, my child. We can talk there.'

I had doubts about following him. I was scared to be alone with him, strange as it may seem. Something about him made me fearful. Nevertheless I followed him out of the nave and into the vestry. He motioned towards a bench where we both sat down.

'So what can I do for you, my child?' he asked with a sly look. 'Have you come for confession?'

'No, I've not come for confession,' I replied, disconcerted by his complete lack of shame at the recollection. I felt annoyed with myself afterwards for not challenging him about his actions back then, but I had to get to the point of my present visit, and I was struggling already to retain my composure.

'Before my mother died,' I continued, 'she tried to say something to me about my father. She said that Filippo

Fiore was not my real father. But she died before she could say who my true father was.'

'I see.'

'Afterwards, I spoke to my brother Luigi.'

'Yes?'

'And he said . . .'

'Yes?'

I swallowed hard.

'He said that you were my father.'

I fixed him with a steady gaze, waiting for his response. I was surprised when he began, slowly and raspingly, to laugh.

'Me, your father? Ha ha ha, that's funny. That's very funny.' He continued to laugh like a drain swallowing water.

'What's funny about it?'

'What's funny is the idea that I could have fathered a child at all. Ha, ha, ha. You see my dear, in all my long life I have never had sex with a woman. Women never interested me, if you know what I mean.'

'So you're not my father. You're definitely not my father?'

'No, Rosa, I'm sorry to disappoint you, but I am not.'

'Oh, I'm not disappointed, Padre,' I said. 'You disgust me.' And with that I walked away.

He was still chuckling to himself as I left the *chiesa* with my heart full of joy on knowing this pervert was not my father. So Luigi had been wrong. He did not know everything. But if neither Filippo Fiore or Padre Francesco were my father, then who in heaven's name was? And if Luigi had been wrong about Mama's infidelity, could he be wrong about l'Inglese? Could he have lied about everything?

As I reached the *fattoria*, Rosario was idling in the yard, kicking up the dirt with the toes of his boots and smoking a pipe, causing clouds of blue smoke to hover above his head.

He limped over at my approach: he had evidently been waiting for me.

'What is it, Rosario? I am very busy and very tired.'

'Rosario talk to Rosa,' he said.

'All right, what is it?'

'Rosario tell Rosa something.'

'Yes?'

'Rosario Rosa's papa.'

Holy Mother of God.

'What do you mean, Rosario? What are you talking about?'

He became flustered and began mumbling incomprehensibly to himself.

'Rosario, come into *la cucina*. Come on. Come and talk to Rosa.'

I took him inside and sat him down at the table with a jug of ale to loosen his brain.

'You said "Rosario Rosa's papa." Now come on, explain it to me. Take your time. Don't be frightened. Just tell me what you mean.'

Rosario rubbed his face with his fingers, which he always did when he felt nervous and was trying to think.

'Come on now,' I said slowly and encouragingly.

'There's no-one here to hear us. Just Rosario and Rosa. Rosario tell Rosa what he knows.'

'Dark night. Cold. Rosario in cowshed. Warm in there, see?'

'Yes . . .'

'Rosario not allowed in cowshed. She said so. But he didn't mean no harm. Warming himself, see?'

'Yes, go on, Rosario, no-one's going to be cross with you.'

'She came in, but I didn't know it was her. It was dark, you see.'

'Yes, it was dark. Go on.'

'She does things to Rosario. It wasn't his fault. He didn't know it was her. He couldn't help it. He didn't mean no wrong.'

'No, he didn't. Go on.'

'Afterwards she lights the lantern. She very angry. She beat Rosario. She whip him. A case of mistaken identity, she say. She tell Rosario if he tell, she lock him away, see? I don't want to be locked away. You won't lock me away, will you?'

'No, Rosario, it's all right. I won't let anything happen to you.'

'Then *bambina* come. Rosario's *bambina*. She say he mustn't know *bambina*. Or love it. He not allowed. He not to touch it or love it or talk to it or Rosario be locked away in a dungeon. But Rosario love Rosa. Always he love Rosa. She gone now. She dead. She can't lock Rosario up now. Rosario Rosa's papa. Rosa Rosario's *bambina*.'

Good God, so this imbecile was my father.

'It's all right, Rosario. No-one is going to hurt you or lock you up or anything like that. I won't let them. Now I

250

need to think carefully about everything, so Rosario, go now and let Rosa think. Everything is going to be all right. I promise you. No harm will come to you. You go and get on with your work. They'll be needing you in the fields.'

He drained his jug of ale and left *la cucina*. When he was gone I banged my head against the table several times, hoping the physical pain would take away the emotional anguish.

I was the daughter of a halfwit. How could my mother have done this to me? I was in no doubt about the truth of his story. As he was talking to me, I was struck by my physical likeness to him; his nose was the same as mine, his eyes the same colour green, his arched eyebrows, his build, his teeth: these things had never struck me before. To tell the truth, I had never really looked at him closely. Also the expressions of his face, his mannerisms, the movements of his hands when talking: it was like looking in a mirror. I had a halfwit for a father. How could things get any worse than this?

I ran to the stove and fried some slabs of *panelle* that I had already prepared for lunch. I crammed the oozing golden fritters into my mouth and kept eating until my rage subsided. I had to remain calm. I had lived through worse tragedies than this one.

CHAPTER NINE

Before I knew it, a year had passed since my return to Castiglione. Now I ran the farm in place of Mama. I had made some changes of which I have to admit I was rather proud. I had introduced a proper bookkeeping system, and recorded my accounts in a series of neatly written ledgers, just like those at the library. I had organized a little office for myself and equipped it with an impressive array of stationery items that I had acquired from the shops at Randazzo. There were sharpened pencils, an assortment of pens, paper, and envelopes in various sizes, labelled files, and rubber stamps. It was all very pleasing.

Yet the changes I made were not purely administrative. I made lots of practical improvements as well. I had the pipes dug to connect the farm to the main water and sewerage systems. I had renovated some cottages on the far side of the estate and had installed Rosario and some of the other farmhands and their families in them. After all, I could not allow my father to live in a hovel.

I had got over my initial depression at discovering my real father's identity. Rosario was slow, but he was a kind and honest man, and I was touched by his devotion to me. The love for me that he was forced to hide while Mama was alive, he now showed in a thousand little ways. He would bring me flowers he had gathered from the hedgerows or a fresh warm egg from his chickens. And he would wash the dishes after mealtimes, gravely ignoring the hilarity of my brothers and the other farm-hands that this caused. Over time he won me over and I grew very fond of him in spite of myself.

I soon bought a tractor, the first one in the region, and a truck to take produce to market. The neighbours said that Mama would be turning in her grave at the expenditure, but they were just jealous. I was convinced that we had to move into the future rather than continue to do things the old-fashioned way.

It was not my intention to take over, but none of my brothers had any idea how to run a business. Every minute one of them would run into *la cucina* asking me what Mama would have done in a given situation, so it came about naturally that I took over all responsibility. I decided which pastures should be used for which of the crops. I determined which of the livestock should be bred and which slaughtered. I settled on what produce should be stored and what sent to market, and so on. There was a long line of strong women in my family and I suppose the men had just never taken the trouble to think for themselves. Oh, for l'Inglese. He was a man in the truest sense of the word.

And yet, for all my added responsibilities, I did not neglect my duties in the kitchen; I like to think that none of my brothers or the farmhands, of which there were an increasing number, had eaten better in their lives. I prepared them breakfast, lunch, and supper. I would produce a huge pot roast or serve a young suckling pig fresh from the sty. I still made all my own bread, and there would often be a handsome dessert or a new cheese and apples.

I was happy, in a way. I didn't have a lover, so I couldn't experience the highs and lows of love. I could only reminisce about the feel of a man inside me; remember my sighs as his stiffened member would gently draw back the layers of my lower lips, and then, having admitted him, would close back around him like the petals of a rose.

L'Inglese was all too often on my mind, particularly when I was in *la cucina*, preparing one of the dishes we had made together. I never could eat spaghetti without smiling at the recollection of that night. I never stopped missing him. Sometimes I fantasized about what would have happened if he hadn't disappeared. Could our love have lasted beyond that glorious summer? I asked myself. Good sense told me he would eventually have gone away, back to his real life in Oxford or London, or one of those other places in England I had read about in a book in the library.

And yet, if he had not gone away, what then? At such times my hands would come to rest in a bowl of steaming dough, my eyes would glaze over, and my imagination would take flight.

Once I saw us on the steps of the duomo, back in Palermo. It was a day in early summer: May, I think, when the light is silver and the breeze still cools. I was wearing the pink two-piece suit I was once so proud of, and a little pillbox hat with a veil. Brightly coloured petals of confetti fluttered in my face, making me laugh. L'Inglese, standing at my side in a smart suit, was smiling his mischievous smile.

We climbed into a waiting chaise and I tossed my bouquet of orange blossoms into the air. All the squealing girls leapt up with their arms outstretched but it was Costanza, the hussy, who caught it.

The library staff, the regular readers, the poor students, they were all there, even the director and the *signora* in an expensive costume. Everyone, except the *signora*, who was too well bred, was laughing and crying and clapping and cheering as we drove away.

I distinctly heard the pony's hooves crunching on the gravel as l'Inglese leaned over and kissed me, his little moustache tickling my lips.

'What's for lunch, Rosa?' he asked.

Only it wasn't l'Inglese. It was Giuliano passing through the kitchen.

I rebuked myself for wasting time daydreaming when I saw that the morning had somehow disappeared. In dismay I realized that the farmhands would soon be coming in for their lunch and the sardines I needed for my *pasta con sarde* wouldn't bone themselves.

Quickly I removed the bones from the mountain of sad-looking sardines lying in front of me on the table. In fact, I like to think I broke all records for boning on this occasion. I removed the heads too, and coated the bodies in a seasoned flour mixture of my own special recipe.

I fried onions in olive oil, added some handfuls of

just-picked fennel leaves and some raisins and pine nuts, and cooked the mixture over a low heat for a few minutes. In a separate pan I fried my now flaccid sardines, while boiling penne in plenty of boiling salted water.

As the farmhands were trooping through the door, stretching out their aching backs and wiping their sweaty brows, I drained the penne, stirred in the fennel mixture, arranged the sardines on the top, and sprinkled the whole with toasted bread crumbs.

Although the lunch wasn't late, this incident taught me a lesson, and I resolved to confine my daydreaming to the times when I was off duty.

CHAPTER TEN

As the months passed in the steady round of managing the farm, the date of Biancamaria Ossobuco's confinement approached, and Guerra and Pace decided they wanted to marry her before their child was born.

They approached Padre Francesco, and he made no objection to marrying the three of them in his church. The date was set for the following week, and a huge flurry of preparations began.

Yards of white silk were hurriedly brought in from the mainland, and the tailor, Banquo Cuniberto, set to work fashioning a silken tent to cover the enormous form of Biancamaria Ossobuco. The twins too were to be arrayed in morning dress in the European style, and Banquo Cuniberto and his assistants worked in relays round the clock to perfect the tailoring of the tailcoat and the three-legged trousers.

I too wanted to have a new costume, and chose a pink two-piece suit, just like the one I had made in Palermo and worn the day when l'Inglese came to the library.

I prepared everything for the wedding breakfast

257

personally. I single-handedly slaughtered a cow so there could be a whole side of beef set out on the table in *la cucina*. In addition, I prepared four different pasta dishes, a decorated swordfish, and a tin bath full of *pollo all Messinese*, a dish traditionally served at weddings.

I also decorated a cake and moulded out of marzipan little coloured figures of Guerra and Pace and Biancamaria Ossobuco in their wedding finery to adorn the top. There were barrels of my home-brewed ale and grappa, and other good things too.

I had given the farmhands the day off to celebrate the wedding. As we processed towards the *chiesa* from the *fattoria*, all dressed in our finest, I felt an enormous sense of pride at how I had managed things at the farm.

Then, when the excitement of the wedding was over, we all waited for the birth of the child. Usually, after I had presided over supper at the *fattoria*, I would ride the mule into town with a basket of food for Biancamaria and the twins.

One evening I had just unpacked a jar of soup, some freshly made macaroni with a lamb ragout, a cured ham with lime pickles, and a dish of tiny new potatoes, when Biancamaria began to clutch her grossly distended stomach in pain and stumbled backward against the kitchen counter. She stepped on her house dog, which emitted a howl of agony.

'Is it time, Biancamaria Ossobuco?' (I could never manage to call her Biancamaria Fiore, I don't know why.) I asked fearfully, without really wanting to hear the answer.

She nodded feebly. I could tell she was terrified. She had swelled so large it was sure to be a multiple birth, and I knew her fear that her child might be cursed in the same way as its fathers.

Her waters had broken and were pouring down her legs onto the floor.

'There now,' I said, leading her slowly and carefully up the stairs to the main bedroom.

'You lie down here while I go and fetch the doctor. Nothing is going to happen before I get back.'

I hurried down the stairs and out into the street, wishing that the twins had not chosen this particular evening to stay away on business in Catania.

I rushed to Dr Leobino's house, which was some way off in the Via Piave. When the maidservant finally came to the door, she told me that the doctor had taken off to an urgent call in Montalbano and was not likely to return until the early hours of the next morning. How I cursed my own fortune and that of Biancamaria Ossobuco as I hurried back to the house. I knew it would be pointless to ask anyone else for help. Biancamaria Ossobuco was shunned by the rest of the town and no woman would risk rousing her man's anger by coming to our aid. Too bad the toothless midwife Margarita Gengiva had perished in a landslide some eighteen years ago.

As I neared the house I could hear Biancamaria Ossobuco's pitiful cries issuing from the open upstairs window.

'Pace, Guerra. *Aiuto! Morio!*'

'It's all right, my dear,' I called, racing up the stairs two at a time. 'No need to panic. I'm here.'

'Where is the doctor?'

'He's coming. He's on his way. He'll just be a little while. And while he's coming we'll just get everything ready.'

I was trying to think what needed to be done, but my mind was like a lump of dough. I had never been at a birth before. Although I could remember the night of the twins' birth, I was kept well away from the birth chamber, and had no idea what had gone on inside. I knew that clean towels and basins of hot water were customary on such occasions, so I busied myself arranging these, and then sat down by Biancamaria Ossobuco, trying to buoy her up with words of encouragement and mopping her sweating brow with a cloth.

Her pain, her breathing, and her cries all deepened. I was really panicking but was determined not to let her see it. She kept asking where the doctor was, and when he was coming. I could see he was not going to arrive in time.

Her contractions came more closely together and I urged her to push and breathe and push again, and then, quite suddenly, a tiny red head emerged between her legs. I took hold of it and pulled gently. A tiny slippery body emerged too, covered with a purple-coloured mucus. Biancamaria Ossobuco strained her neck to see.

'Is it joined, Rosa?' she whispered, as if scared to speak out loud for fear of knowing the answer.

'No, dear. It's a beautiful baby girl. Look!'

I held the baby up for Biancamaria Ossobuco to see. She was a sweet little thing. Like a piglet. I knew that I had to cut the string that still bound her to her mother, so I took a sharp knife and sliced through it, close to the baby's stomach. And then I took her and washed her in the basin to remove the slime, and dried her carefully. As I turned to hand her to her mother I was amazed to see another little head poking out.

'Biancamaria Ossobuco, I think it's twins. Don't panic. You take hold of this one while I get the other one out.'

I could tell that Biancamaria Ossobucco was still in fear that the second baby could somehow be joined to the first, and she examined the first one all over for some evidence of abnormality. She continued to look fearful while I eased the second one out of the birth canal. The second one, also, was perfectly formed.

'There dear, another one, just like the first, no marks or blemishes at all.'

Again I cut the string, washed the baby, dried it, and wrapped it up to keep it warm. I gave it to Biancamaria Ossobuco and she balanced one of them in either arm, scarcely believing her good fortune. The poor woman had convinced herself that her babies would be deformed, and she did not want to congratulate herself too soon in case the Fates changed their minds.

I bustled around and cleaned everything up, satisfied at the way that I had managed it all. After all, I had no experience, and delivering babies is no easy matter.

As I raised the sheets to wash Biancamaria Ossobuco, you will not believe it if I tell you that there was yet another child seeking to force its way out into the world. Another tiny head was protruding from between

Biancamaria Ossobuco's legs. The poor wretch was in such a state of confusion and relief that she had not realized that she was still in labour.

It was another girl, identical to the first two. This time I took the precaution of poking around Biancamaria Ossobuco's belly, and felt reasonably confident that this was the last.

'Can you feel any more inside you, dear?' I asked her.

'No, Rosa. There will be no more. That was the last one.'

And so my nieces were born. Three of them. All of them identical. All of them beautiful. And delivered by their aunt.

In the early hours, after the excitement had died down and Biancamaria Ossobuco and her triplets had fallen asleep, I took refuge in the kitchen, and sought to calm my nerves by making a pan of *panelle*. There was still nothing like it for soothing my soul and easing my conscience. As I fried the slabs of chickpea paste in crackling hot oil, the twins and the doctor came in together.

'Is she all right?' the boys asked as I gestured the doctor up the stairs. Their four eyes were filled with the same look of fear as Biancamaria Ossobuco's had been a few hours earlier – the fear of passing on their legacy of deformity to their unborn child.

'She's fine, boys,' I answered. 'And you have three beautiful, separate daughters.'

'Then they're all all right? And Biancamaria Ossobuco?'

'They're fine. She's fine. They're all fine. They really are. Go up and look at them.'

They leapt on their three legs up the stairs. I followed and saw their tears of joy on beholding their beautiful family of girls. It was one of the happiest moments of my life.

That night was three years ago now, and today I am in *la cucina* at the *fattoria* minding my nieces, Rosa, Rosita, and Rosina. True to their word, the twins named all three of them after me. They come to me often. They are happy with me. I love them tenderly. They are like my own girls. I am the only one who can tell them apart; even their parents sometimes make mistakes.

I never knew I had such a deep, encompassing ability to love. These three tiny girls have brought me to life again. I give them all the love I have inside me: I have nowhere else to give it now.

And something else too. They are all, even at this tender age, excellent cooks like their aunt Rosa. They are never happier than when they are in the kitchen, covered in flour up to their tiny elbows, kneading miniature dough balls, forming pasta shapes with their baby fingers, or making little biscuits, which they distribute among their favourite farmhands.

I am helping baby Rosa, the eldest, to make 'little oranges': fritters made from rice and three types of cheese. Now that we have boiled the arborio rice in water until tender, drained it, and let it cool, we mix it with mashed ricotta, grated pecorino, chopped mozzarella, parsley, egg, nutmeg, and salt and pepper.

With wet hands we form the mixture into balls. This can be a messy procedure, especially for a three-year-old, and baby Rosa and I are caked in the gloop, which she is happily smearing on both our faces with her teeny fingers. I can't help but laugh, which encourages her to do it all the more. However hard I try, I can't be strict with my girls.

What few balls remain we roll in flour, beaten egg, and lastly bread crumbs. As I set the oil to heat on the stove I glance over the top of the half door, out onto the yard.

The light is so intense at this, the height of summer, that my eyes water as they struggle to adjust to the brightness. In the glare I think I see a figure walking up the lane towards the gate. Something about this figure interests me, I don't know what. Something about it speaks to me, and draws me to it. I squint my eyes trying to make out who it is.

It is the figure of a man. I recognize the figure, and the walk, and the bearing from a distance. Then I wipe my eyes on my sleeve and tell myself I am imagining things. I have not had a daydream for a very long time. I must have grown out of them as I have got older. Nevertheless, I remove the oil from the heat. My fantasies had already been responsible for one fire. My concern for the safety of my nieces has become instinctive.

When I cross to the door and look again, the man is

still there. Closer. Clearer. More definite. I wipe my
hands on my apron and lift little Rosa down from the
table onto the floor, where her sisters are playing with a
kitten. She protests loudly; she wants to continue cooking. For the first time, Aunt Rosa does not listen and
baby Rosa howls.

The air seems to have grown thick around me. I am
conscious of the girls' voices babbling in the background,
the mewing of the over-loved kitten, the smell on my
hands of freshly chopped parsley. But all of that seems
very far away now. I feel like a sleepwalker, or a deep-sea
diver, far away from everything except the bubble of
joy expanding in my heart, which I am struggling to
suppress. Don't let me be dreaming this, I hear my voice
saying inside my mind, I'll die if it isn't real.

My legs walk me towards the door. My arms reach out
and release the catch. I shut the door behind me so the
girls can't get out and fall down the steps. They start
crying because they don't want to be left behind.

I feel the shock of the sudden heat as I emerge from
the cool air of *la cucina* into the full force of the sun. I
come down the steps. My legs feel unsteady, as if they
can't really support my weight. I want to fly, dance, sing,
cry, scream.

I cup my hand over my eyes to shade them so I can see
better, and I realize my face is still caked with the rice
and cheese mixture. But I can't worry about that now.
The figure of the man is standing at the gate, leaning on it
with his forearms, waiting for me. I feel his eyes on me.
They're blue and sparkling as ever.

'Have I come to the right place, signorina?' he asks in

an English accent, his rakish smile lighting up his face and my world.

'You have,' I answer, and my voice sounds from somewhere strangely far off.

THE END

NECTAR

Lily Prior

By the author of *La Cucina*, a new novel set in Italy about a
servant girl whose bewitching aroma drives men who inhale
it into an erotic frenzy.

Ramona Drottoveo, an albino with unusual looks, is a
chambermaid at a lush Italian country estate. Distinguished
by an intoxicating scent, Ramona is despised by all women
and worshipped by all men, whose inexhaustible lust she
eagerly satisfies.

But Ramona's life changes forever when she marries a sweet
beekeeper who dies after discovering his bride with a new
lover on their wedding day. The superstitious villagers blame
Ramona when his body mysteriously disappears, and exile
the couple from the estate. The story follows Ramona's
tragicomic misadventures in the neighbouring city of Naples,
where her life is transformed once again by the birth of an
unwanted daughter, Blandina.

A hilarious and naughty celebration of the senses and the
strange places they can lead us. *Nectar* explores, with a touch of
magical realism, the mystery of sexual attraction, the instinct to
survive and the frivolous nature of divine justice.

0 552 77088 4

BLACK SWAN

LIKE WATER FOR CHOCOLATE

A Novel in Monthly Instalments with Recipes, Romances and Home Remedies

Laura Esquivel

'THIS MAGICAL, MYTHICAL, MOVING STORY OF LOVE, SACRIFICE AND SIMMERING SENSUALITY IS SOMETHING I SHALL SAVOUR FOR A LONG TIME'
Maureen Lipman

The number one bestseller in Mexico for almost two years, and subsequently a bestseller around the world, *Like Water for Chocolate* is a romantic, poignant tale, touched with moments of magic, graphic earthiness and bittersweet wit. A sumptuous feast of a novel, it relates the bizarre history of the all-female De La Garza family. Tita, the youngest daughter of the house, has been forbidden to marry, condemned by Mexican tradition to look after her mother until she dies. But Tita falls in love with Pedro, and in desperation he marries her sister Rosaura so that he can stay close to her. For the next 22 years Tita and Pedro are forced to circle each other in unconsummated passion. Only a freakish chain of tragedies, bad luck and fate finally reunite them against all the odds.

'WONDERFUL . . . HARD TO PUT DOWN . . . IT IS RARE TO COME ACROSS A BOOK AS UNUSUAL'
Steve Vines, *South China Morning Post*

'A TALL-TALE, FAIRY-TALE, SOAP-OPERA ROMANCE, MEXICAN COOKBOOK AND HOME-REMEDY HANDBOOK ALL ROLLED INTO ONE . . . IF ORIGINALITY, A COMPELLING TALE AND AN ADVENTURE IN THE KITCHEN ARE WHAT YOU CRAVE, *LIKE WATER FOR CHOCOLATE* SERVES UP THE FULL HELPING'
Carla Matthews, *San Francisco Chronicle*

The worldwide bestseller — now a major film.

0 552 99587 8

BLACK SWAN

THE HOUSE OF THE SPIRITS

Isabel Allende

Spanning four generations, Isabel Allende's magnificent family saga is populated by a memorable, often eccentric cast of characters. Together, men and women, spirits, the forces of nature, and of history, converge in an unforgettable, wholly absorbing and brilliantly realized novel which is as richly entertaining as it is a masterpiece of modern literature.

'A REMARKABLE ACHIEVEMENT ... A BIG BOOK THAT CAN COMPREHEND THE HISTORY OF A NATION, AND SO MANY LIVES, WITH LOVE'
The Times, London

'THIS IS A NOVEL LIKE THE NOVELS NO-ONE SEEMS TO WRITE ANYMORE: THICK WITH PLOT AND BRISTLING WITH CHARACTERS WHO PLAY OUT THEIR LIVES OVER THREE GENERATIONS OF CONFLICT AND RECONCILIATION. A NOVEL TO BE READ FOR ITS BRILLIANT CRAFTSMANSHIP AND ITS NARRATIVE OF INIESCAPABLE POWER'
El Pais, Madrid

'ANNOUNCING A TRULY GREAT READ: A NOVEL THICK AND THRILLING, FULL OF FANTASY, TERROR AND WIT, ELABORATELY CRAFTED YET SERIOUS AND ACCURATE IN ITS HISTORICAL AND SOCIAL OBSERVATIONS'
Die Welt, Berlin

Now a major film directed by Bille August and starring Meryl Streep, Glenn Close, Jeremy Irons, Winona Ryder, Vanessa Redgrave, Antonio Banderas and Keaunu Reeves.

0 552 99588 6

BLACK SWAN

THE MISTRESS OF SPICES

Chitra Banerjee Divakaruni

'A DAZZLING TALE OF MISBEGOTTEN DREAMS AND
DESIRES, HOPES AND EXPECTATIONS, WOVEN WITH
POETRY AND STORYTELLER MAGIC'
Amy Tan

'A MARVELLOUS COMBINATION OF MYTH AND
ROMANCE, SOCIAL CRITIQUE AND POETRY'
San Francisco Chronicle

Tilo, an immigrant from India, runs a spice shop in Oakland,
California. While she supplies the ingredients for curries and kormas,
she also helps her customers to gain a more precious commodity:
whatever they most desire. For Tilo is a Mistress of Spices, a priestess
of the secret magical powers of spices.

Through those who visit and revisit her shop, she catches glimpses of
the life of the local Indian expatriate community. To each, Tilo
dispenses wisdom and the appropriate spice, for the restoration of
sight, the cleansing of evil, the pain of rejection. But when a lonely
American ventures into the store, a troubled Tilo cannot find the
correct spice, for he arouses in her a forbidden desire – which if she
follows will destroy her magical powers . . .

'DIVAKARUNI'S MAGIC [IS] HER ABILITY TO CRAFT SUCH
A COMPLEX TALE WRITTEN SO EXQUISITELY WITHOUT
OVERWHELMING HER READER'
Los Angeles Times

'FASCINATING STUFF . . . APPEALINGLY FLAVOURED AND
COLOURFUL'
Mail on Sunday

'A SPLENDID NOVEL, BEAUTIFULLY CONCEIVED AND
CRAFTED. THIS BOOK IS SO GOOD THAT I WANT TO
READ EVERYTHING SHE HAS WRITTEN BEFORE AND
EVERYTHING SHE WILL EVER WRITE IN THE FUTURE'
Pat Conroy

0 552 99670 X

BLACK SWAN

A SELECTED LIST OF FINE WRITING
AVAILABLE FROM BLACK SWAN

THE PRICES SHOWN BELOW WERE CORRECT AT THE TIME OF GOING TO
PRESS. HOWEVER TRANSWORLD PUBLISHERS RESERVE THE RIGHT TO
SHOW NEW RETAIL PRICES ON COVERS WHICH MAY DIFFER FROM THOSE
PREVIOUSLY ADVERTISED IN THE TEXT OR ELSEWHERE.

All Transworld titles are available by post from:
Bookpost, P.O. Box 29, Douglas, Isle of Man IM99 1BQ
Credit cards accepted. Please telephone 01624 836000,
fax 01624 837033, Internet http://www.bookpost.co.uk.
or e-mail: bookshop@enterprise.net for details

Free postage and packing in the UK.
Overseas customers: allow £1 per book.